The Occidental Husband

A man with one chopstick is
always one shy of a full load.

The practically unbelievable, curiously true story of
a Western man, an Eastern woman, and the fate of mankind
(or at least one little boy).

Fred L. Smith

Published by
Evening Post Books
134 Columbus Street
Charleston, South Carolina
29403
Copyright © 2013 by Fred Smith

Editors: John M. Burbage/Holly Holladay
Designer: Gill Guerry
Author photo: Grace Beahm

First printing 2013
Printed in the United States of America

A CIP catalog record for this book has been applied
for from the Library of Congress.

ISBN: 978-1-929647-15-6

For Connor

PREFACE

"Remember, Fred, you asked for this."

That's what I kept telling myself. I *asked* to marry a Chinese woman. I *asked* her to take me out of my simple, rural existence in a place called Goose Creek, South Carolina to the captivating conundrum that is China. I *asked* to be standing — no, make that *squatting* — in a bathroom train heading north from Beijing at four in the morning, swaying back and forth, full of exotic liquors and trying to *crap through a hole in the floor*!

But this was not exactly how I envisioned my life a year earlier when I went online trying to find a wife. Everyone said I was nutty looking for romance on the Internet (this was the '90s and online dating was very new). Nuttier, even, to get entangled with a foreigner who might be using me just to get a green card.

I first made contact with Mei in 1997, the same year the British-held Hong Kong rejoined China, but I think that was just a coincidence. She had never held a puppy, never walked on the beach, never eaten a hot dog, or watched a Three Stooges pie fight.

She had much to learn and experience. But I had no idea I would do most of the learning ... and all of the growing up. For me, the road to enlightenment was paved with strange relatives, weird food, and miscommunication mishaps. I found I would have to change my attitude to *win* Mei, then change again on a more profound level to *keep* Mei, only to learn that, ultimately, nothing is "for keeps."

As Mei embarked on her own journey of discovery in a strange environment miles from her unique world in the Far East, she helped transform me from a geeky loser into something resembling a responsible family man.

I have to admit, though, that many times I felt like a man with one chopstick: just one shy of a full load.

ONE
DON'T DATE YOUR AUNT

"Mom, I'm going to marry a Chinese immigrant I met on the Internet," I proclaimed in June of 1997.

My mom's dentures popped out of her startled mouth, fell, and broke on the hardwood floor of my living room. And those were her fancy eatin' teeth.

Sure, the news came as a shock. However, since I was forty-two years old and didn't even date that much, I think the shock waves were probably tempered with a sense of relief. I must say my mom was in the beginning stages of senile dementia, a condition partly brought on by having me as an off-spring. So she probably thought this was not actually happening.

But what sane man would marry a woman he met on the Internet and had known for only *six weeks*?

Hey, did I mention anything about sanity?

A noted philosopher, I think it was Richard Pryor, once said: "Horny makes ya brave." I would add that "love makes you crazy." And in 1997, it was considered somewhat crazy to hook up online. To quote Tony Curtis in "Some Like it Hot" (referring to two men running off together in the 1930s): "It just isn't being done."

But let's go back a few months prior to my wacky wedding announcement. At that time I lived a quiet life in Goose Creek, a small city just north of Charleston, South Carolina. My family moved from Charleston to Goose Creek in 1968 when I was thirteen. I attended Goose Creek High School, where I made all As. Certainly not because I was smart; because the school was so poor at the time, it could only afford one letter.

By 1997 I had been working at *The Post and Courier* (previously, *The News and Courier*), the South's oldest daily newspaper, for seventeen years: first as a paste-up man, then copy editor, TV columnist, movie critic, and finally a page designer (I couldn't settle on one job because I wasn't brilliant at any of them).

I had moved back in with my mom, one Doris Smith, after my dad died in '84 — leaving her, unfortunately, with nothing except the knowledge that her husband and the father of her three children had committed suicide — and in '91, she moved in with me after I bought a small house in my old stomping grounds of Goose Creek.

Living with Mom made life, for me at least, certainly not for her, easy and uncomplicated. Perhaps *too* easy and uncomplicated. It took a thing called the World Wide Web to shake things up. But, boy, I was in such a rut that I *needed* shaking up.

To set the record straight, I'm not a computer geek. Geek? Yeah. Computer geek? No. This is nothing to brag about, for being a "regular" geek like me is worse than being a computer geek. At least a computer geek can play cool video games and maybe get a high-paying job fixing systems or whatever those guys do. But as a regular geek, all I can do is answer some useless trivia questions, like:

Q: Who was the Lone Ranger's great-great-great nephew?

A: The Green Hornet. They were both created by George W. Trendle, as surely everyone knows.

Otherwise, I'm fairly useless.

Unfortunately, computers have always frustrated and confused me. For decades I believed they were out to get me. Them … and squirrels.

But, as a means to an end, I bought a computer to get on this new wonder (remember this is happening in the last century) called the Internet for the sole purpose of finding a wife.

I realized in my early forties that I was still playing little boy games, and I knew it was time to grow up, especially since I was still watching Godzilla movies and collecting comic books. These things are great but ultimately unfulfilling.

In no way was I a typical Southerner. To me, a typical Southerner might fish on Lake Moultrie. He might do a dance called the Shag. He might drive a truck. He might barbecue. He might watch NASCAR. All those things are fine, but I didn't do any of them. The most redneck thing I did was play softball.

I was a certified late bloomer, having once led a sheltered life (the reasons for this are detailed in the next chapter), and I was eager to experience what had been missing in my life: a wife, some kids, and — dare I say it — a minivan! Besides, I was ready to come out of the persistent vegetative state more commonly known as watching too much television.

I took the Internet route for several reasons:

#1: I didn't like the bar scene. Not because they are bad places but because I'm the kind of guy who gets beaten up and robbed there — by women.

#2: I didn't do the church bit. I've heard the best place to meet classy chicks is in church, but pews are uncomfortable places for sex.

#3: I didn't like dating services. I tried one, before they all went online, but apparently I didn't make it clear to the people who were matching me up that I wanted to date within my own species.

#4: Forging intimate relationships at the newspaper office presented its own peculiar pitfalls. There was the gruesome legend about the two reporters who were making out in the pressroom and fell into one of the rollers. It gave new meaning to the printer's term "spot red." But I digress … .

I also had a problem asking women out. My approach was a bit unusual: I made them fill out a three-page application form listing age, weight, bank account balances, and next of kin in case of an "accident." For some reason, this turned women off.

So the Internet seemed a quick and convenient way for me to meet available women and get all the facts up front. After much weeping, wailing, and gnashing of teeth, I finally got online and hit the singles sites, which were proliferating even in '97.

I felt if I couldn't find a decent woman (i.e. a sexpot who could stomach me) on the 'net, I would renew my subscription to Playboy and return to my late-night dates in the bathroom with self.

Before I found my future wife, I met two other women online and those experiences — one harrowing, the other hedonistic — deserve mention.

It was March of '97 when I contacted a woman in Florida, just two states away, to whom I shall refer as Ezmirelda Van Klumpp (not her real name). Van Klumpp and I exchanged about a hundred e-mails, and she seemed perfect for me. We were about the same age. We had many of the same likes and dislikes. She was intelligent. I was intelligent. She had just come out of a bad relationship. I had just come out of a bad relationship. She wore black panties. I wore black panties (well, once, after those four martinis).

We were truly compatible, or so it seemed. I poured out my heart to her — as well as most of my brain stem — and our e-mails were getting more and more passionate. Finally, we braved a phone conversation. I should have grown suspicious right then because her voice sounded a bit husky. But I just kept thinking of Kathleen Turner. Yeah, I was that desperate!

After several more nights of hot e-mails, without even having set eyes on each other, we declared our love. I felt I was intellectually deep enough to love someone without much regard to her physical appearance. (*Wrong*! I was just as shallow and stupid as any man. Stupider, even.)

Still, we weren't idiots willing to jump off any cliff. We decided it was a good idea to exchange pictures before meeting. Of course, this was long before Facebook. Trading pics was to be done the old-fashioned way, via something called "The United States Postal Service."

Instead of a picture though, I made a short video of myself — on something called "VHS tape" — with my best friend Mark Grahn's camcorder. Mark and I lived in the same neighborhood. We shared some important and thought-provoking interests such as *Spider-Man*, *Popeye* (the old black and whites, we were true connoisseurs), the Carolina Panthers, the Beatles, *Seinfeld*, and naturally, our cold fusion experiments.

Van Klumpp received the video and said to me on the phone: "I have met my dream man!"

Again, this was a clue I missed. Frankly, my video was *not* good. The fact that she loved it proved that this was a woman who was *not* used to getting offers.

Then, I received a photo of her. I was extremely disappointed. She didn't look like Quasimodo, but a *Sports Illustrated* swimsuit model she was not.

However, I owed it to her, and to myself, to give her a chance. After all, some people don't photograph well. Maybe she looked a lot better in person. And maybe Mickey Dolenz and Davy Jones might fly out of my butt! (Obscure Monkees reference that you old-timers will appreciate.)

We decided to meet each other half way between our homes, at a hotel in Savannah, Georgia.

Meanwhile, my colleagues at work were extremely curious about my escapades. They were used to my antics in the office, at least in my younger days. I was the guy who took one of those little pink chewables the dentist gives you to highlight the areas of plaque on your teeth and gave it to a sweet but gullible reporter named Vicki, pretending it was candy. Well, she chewed it up, leaving the hard-to-brush-off pink stains smeared all over her teeth, and she had to do an interview in an hour. Everyone thought it was funny except poor Vicki. But don't blame me for this. It was Vicki's fault for not brushing properly.

Anyway, before I left work on Friday to meet my

one false love, I hatched a plan with Ellen Anderson, a fellow copy editor. Once I arrived at the hotel, I was supposed to call Ellen to tell her that I had arrived safely. But the real reason for the call was to give a "yea" or "nay" on this woman. If I thought she was okay, I would say the code word "one" to Ellen. If she was a dog, I was supposed to say "two." And if my romantic well-being was in extreme danger, I would shout "three."

Van Klumpp arrived at the hotel first. She got a room and left the number with the desk clerk (remember we're living in the Stone Age before cell phones). I arrived a bit later and proceeded, nervously, to the room with flowers and condom in hand.

I knocked on the door. She opened it. My first thought was, *Quasimodo lives!!!!*

It turns out the picture she had sent me was probably the best photo ever taken of her: a real "glamour" shot. I hate to be harsh, but in the flesh, she…er…well, let's just say she was not my type. Her body was masculine and misshapen. The "perfume" she was wearing reeked of an old shoe. And, worst of all, she reminded me of a crummy aunt who used to visit my family from upstate when I was a child.

I have done some strange things in my life, but one thing my pappy taught me was this: Never date an aunt.

My only option was to hit the road. Flee. Split the scene. Get the hell outta Dodge. But *hold it*! This woman knew too much about me! She knew where I lived and where I worked! She knew secrets I had never told anyone else! (Like the time when I was a teenager, and I had too much to drink and woke up naked in my next-door neighbor's doghouse as his German Shepherd was licking my — *wait a minute*! I shouldn't be saying this here!)

I thought to myself, *Obviously, if this Van Klumpp woman is meeting someone she found on the Internet in a strange hotel room, she's mentally unstable! What am I going to do?*

It was as if God said to me, "Fred, since you don't seem to believe in me, I'm going to give you small sample of Hell."

First, I called Ellen. But I was so flabbergasted I forgot which code word was which.

Me: "El, I'm here."

Ellen: "So which is it?"

Me: "Huh?"

Ellen: "You forgot, didn't you?"

Me: "Yeah."

Ellen: "'One' if good, 'two' if bad, 'three' if doomed."

Me: "Oh, how about a *four*?!"

I hung up. So what next? What do you do when a refugee from *The Addams Family* puts her arms around you and appears ready for a lip lock? Suddenly, all that "love" talk in our e-mails seemed stupid and embarrassing. How did I get myself into this ridiculous situation?

Well, I knew how! This incident officially made me a ridiculous person.

I had to think. I could have just told her we needed to cool the romance, that we should just spend the weekend getting to know each other. Separate beds. Separate checks. Separate countries. I'll call you.

But, still being something of a selfish bastard, I didn't want to waste even one weekend on her! And yet, having at least some compassion for others, I didn't want to hurt her feelings by telling her she was repulsive.

We talked for a while, and she soon sensed my apprehension. As I sat uncomfortably with her on the couch, she asked me what was wrong, and I then decided on a course of action. Believe it or not, I used an old *Seinfeld* gimmick. I remembered on the show when George started crying in front of a woman to get out of a marriage, or something to that effect. Since I felt like crying anyway — I had pinned my future on this woman, and now my hopes were dashed, plus I was missing that *Gilligan's Island* marathon on Nick at Nite, I decided to release the floodgates and see what happened. I have always been able to cry easily. All I have to do is think of what life would have been like if Stan Lee had never been born and I blubber.

So I started sobbing, telling her I wasn't ready for commitment and I was not the man she thought I was. And you know what? It worked! I knew those years of TV watching would pay off. She consoled me and told me I had problems. (Imagine that … me, problems? Ha!) She started psychoanalyzing me, saying I was still that nine-year-old boy who had his first panic attack. (*Foreshadowing alert!*) This kind of penetrating perception was one of the things that attracted me to Van Klumpp in the first place. Now she was using it against me. Oh, the irony!

We did spend the night together, though of course

nothing happened. But I got a good enough glimpse of her bare chest to confirm all my fears. She had more hair on hers than I had on mine!

The next morning, we parted company. The last thing she said to me was, "You never even gave me a chance."

I felt terrible. I came off like a pathetic jerk, but at least I didn't destroy her by telling her the truth. And, like Larry of the Three Stooges, I managed to retain my dignity.

When I got back to *The Post and Courier* the following Monday, the entire office gathered around me to find out what happened. I could have lied. I could have said Van Klumpp looked like Demi Moore and that her sister was even better looking, and the three of us partied all night, and then they paid me a million dollars. (Jeez, who am I, Beaver Cleaver?)

A failing of mine is that I am always compelled tell the truth, unless it involves bodily harm or money, no matter how foolish it makes me look. And I did not spare the details.

Most of my co-workers probably thought "well, that's typical Fred," and this incident would certainly cure me from trying to find another online bride.

But I wasted no time getting back on the Internet. I had learned some valuable lessons from my first experience, dang it! From now on, I would insist on a picture, and a DNA sample, long before any talk of romance. And I would ask her how many places on her body needed shaving.

We all know this now about e-mail: It is very fast and very seductive. You can learn more about a person from one evening of e-mails than you can a whole month of dating. With e-mails, you're not face-to-face, so all barriers are removed. You can reveal yourself completely without shame or shyness. If you're a neo-Nazi-transvestite-prostitute-drug addict with a fondness for small rodents and toilet water, you can just say it!

Also, all modesty aside, I have earned my living as a writer. A few poetic e-mails from me can accomplish a lot with a needy woman.

So it was no surprise that the second woman I contacted, Mavis Meatmeister (not her real name), fell quickly under the spell of this Internet Casanova. At 6 p.m., she would not even give me her last name. By 8 p.m. I had her full name, address, and phone number. By midnight, we were making love in my bed.

Yep, I went against my own advice and didn't ask for a picture. Taking a chance that she did not resemble a man-ish aunt, I picked up Miss Meatmeister at her, uh, trailer, and drove her to my place. Luckily for me, she was none too bright. Luckily for her, I was not a sexual predator.

It turned out this girl was young, blonde, blue-eyed, and buxom. She was not pretty. But, as I said, she was young, blonde, blue-eyed, and buxom. (Is there any part of this that isn't clear?)

But this time it was my turn to take the fall. You see, she was twenty-eight and sexually active. I was forty-two and had not had sex in a year! (Doesn't everyone go a year between sexual encounters?) My muscles had atrophied! I was out of condition! She kept asking me, "What's the matter?" I didn't reply, but I was thinking, *Hell, I'm about to pass out!*

Also, I was nervous, and without going into details, let's just say it did not go well. I asked her if she would give me another chance. She indicated she would, though I grew suspicious when she declined a ride home, preferring to walk the fifteen miles.

As expected, Miss Meatmeister didn't return my subsequent e-mails, so I spent several nights in the fetal position.

Still, I realized this Internet thing had some wild possibilities. It could be one big sex fest, if that was what one wanted. But I didn't lose sight of my mission: to find a wife. The heck with fun!

Enter Mei Li.

T W O
THE CHINESE CONNECTION

I contacted a few more women in April of '97. Nothing worked out. One was bald. Another weighed 250 pounds. Another I met in a restaurant. She was gorgeous. But I don't think she liked me because when I returned from the restroom, I noticed she had cordoned herself off with yellow police tape. Then I answered the ad that changed my life.

It was April 24. I saw a rather nondescript entry on americansingles.com.

A Chinese lady named Mei in Greenville, S.C., about 200 miles away, was looking for someone to help her with her English and potentially, get married. I was more interested in the second part of that.

I had always fantasized about hooking up with an Asian. Though the ugliest Chinese women are uglier than the ugliest American women, the most beautiful Chinese women are more beautiful than the most beautiful American women. (I've gone over that sentence twenty-seven times, and it still makes sense to me.)

There was a short delay, but she answered me on May 5. It was the beginning of more than three hundred e-mails.

Some stats on Mei:

Full name: Mei Li.

Age: Thirty-three (Born in the Year of the Dragon.)

Profession: Nurse in China.

Religious/Party affiliation: A non-practicing Buddhist; not a member of the Communist Party

Marital status: Divorced

Reason: Husband was abusive.

"Baggage": One daughter, age nine, still in China

Situation: Came to the U.S. one year ago to help "cousin-sister" with new baby and to look for a new life

Characteristics: Sweet, charming, hard-working, but emotionally fragile.

My emails to Mei took about twenty minutes to write, multiple pages. For her, having only been in the country for a year, it routinely took two hours to write a page, dictionary in hand. That was with the help of Susan, the "cousin-sister" (don't ask me how that works). In the midst of this correspondence, she got a passionate e-mail from me, but Susan was on a business trip in Los Angeles. The only other person in the house was George, Susan's husband, an American much like myself except that he was taller, thinner, younger, better looking, and had more money. So, in order to give me a quick response, Mei called Susan in L.A. and had George read her my email (if I had known, I wouldn't have put in that stuff about my midget fetish); Susan then translated the email in Chinese to Mei; then Mei gave her answer to Susan, in Chinese; then Susan gave George the English version, and George then typed it in for Mei. Whew! But there must have been something lost in translation, as Mei referred to me as "Thumper" for the next week.

Mei came across as smart, devoted to her family, and quite innocent. She wrote that she thought it was wonderful that my mom lived with me, for that was the way of things in China. The way she constructed sentences was cute, calling me "good for an American son."

We were both totally honest with each other in our e-mails. It would have served no long-range purpose to try to deceive ourselves. We could lie all we wanted *after* we got married. We revealed ourselves to each other, warts and all. One of the things that attracted Mei to me was that I did not portray myself as Brad Pitt. She knew she was getting just a more-or-less average guy, and it made her feel relaxed and safe. *Hahahahahahahaaa!* (Evil laugh.)

In one email particularly, one of the few which survives, I wanted to reveal to Mei a problem with which I have had to cope most of my life. It sums up why I wasn't married at forty-two and how my dream of having a "normal" life was denied me until I was in my thirties.

Here is that email in full:

May 8, 1997

Mei, my life really started 10 years ago. That's when I began to escape the demons that plagued me since childhood.

I suffer from panic attacks. I now have them under control, through medication, but for most of my life I couldn't even admit the problem.

I had my first panic attack in a restaurant when I was 9 years old. I wanted to order more food, and my father unthinkingly threatened to beat me if I didn't eat all the extra food. I then began to feel ill and couldn't seem to swallow. I didn't know it was a panic attack. I don't think the phrase had even been coined then. I only knew I couldn't eat, and I was terrified.

Of course, my father didn't beat me. He was basically a good man, and had he known his words would trigger something awful inside me, he would never have said them. In fact, his ultimate suicide in 1984 might have partially been due to his guilt over this incident, which dramatically altered the course of my life.

From then on, I associated that first attack with restaurants, and every time the family went out to eat, I got sick. Gradually, the problem spread to other social events. It got to where I was afraid of being anywhere that having an attack would embarrass me. So I avoided those situations.

Anytime a girl would express interest in me, I would have to walk away, because I couldn't take the chance that she would see me having an attack.

We now know that panic attacks are caused by a chemical imbalance in the brain. But as a kid I only knew I was weak, and I was the only person in the world with this problem. My family never talked about it. Ignoring it was easier, which was the worst thing they could have done.

Eventually, the attacks spread to so many areas of my life that the only place I felt comfortable was in the home. I had to drop out of college. Somehow, I managed to get a good job at a newspaper, first in production, then I worked my way up to TV columnist, film critic, and copy editor. I developed a sort of twisted sense of humor to attract attention away from the real me. Everyone thought I was a character, but while I was laughing in the day, I was crying in the night.

For the most part, my life consisted of going to work and coming home and going to movies, alone.

Eventually I developed severe dental problems, but I was unable to do anything about them.

Life was without hope, and I just gave up. I made a half-hearted attempt at suicide in 1984 but obviously failed. Ironically, six weeks later my father did kill himself, no longer able to endure the hardships life heaped on him, which were worse than anything I ever went through.

He left my mom penniless, and suffering from debilitating arthritis, she couldn't work long hours. Since my brother and sister had their own worries and lived out of state, I moved in with her, so we could help each other. Then we sold that house and its tragic memories and I bought a home of my own, and of course brought my mom with me.

Later I learned that other people have panic attacks, and they could be helped through therapy and/or medication. Then I did the bravest thing in my life: I tried to help myself live. After various doctors and several medications, the panic attacks and the depression they brought on began to lift.

I found the right medication to get rid of the physical symptoms of the attacks, but I still had to deal with the mental aspects: the long years of built-up fears. Slowly, through de-synthesization, I was able to go to those places, restaurants included, that I avoided for years. I learned to manage my problem.

Then I did the second most courageous thing: I faced the long-delayed dental surgery. It was an ordeal, but once my teeth were fixed, I began to enjoy the world in ways I never thought possible. I have dated and had relationships, but as yet I haven't found a life partner.

Well, that's my story. You should also know that my mom still lives with me, but she is a great lady, and she wants nothing but my happiness. I'm also height challenged: I'm 5'6" with heels (or nice people).

So you're a foreigner with a 9-year-old daughter,
and I'm a short guy with a 67-year-old mom. Do
you think we can make this work?

Mei replied, saying my email brought tears to her eyes. She was happy I overcame my fears and said that she was the kind of person who would be there for me through all the ups and downs in life. She also assured me she was not seeking to get married just for a green card. She simply wanted to find love and a good home.

Eventually, we exchanged pictures. I liked the way Mei looked except that she wasn't smiling. But I told her I would make her smile.

Meanwhile, Mei received my picture and said it looked okay. In truth, she didn't like it. It was a bad Polaroid shot with half my face in the shadows, and I was wearing one of my famous polyester shirts, a situation Mei later rectified. But she was willing to give me the benefit of the doubt, just as I gave Van Klumpp months earlier.

I wrote her that I believed the cultural gap between us could be bridged with understanding, tolerance, communication, and love. And money.

I wrote that I wanted her to experience the things I like about America and everything it has to offer. At the time, the American economy was booming. It was before 9/11, and the United States the envy of the world. China, meanwhile, was undergoing growing pains, and began to shrug its Atlas-like shoulders.

She told me how difficult those first days in America were, how lonely she was and how she missed her daughter. She came from a close family. Her father was a math professor, and her mom was beautiful, sweet, and warm. Mei left her daughter, Dan Dan, with them when she traveled to South Carolina. She also spoke highly of her three brothers.

We agreed to meet the next Saturday in Greenville. And so I prepared for another meeting with a woman I found on the Internet. But this one felt different. It felt right.

THREE
MEETING MEI

It's not very romantic, but I swear I first saw Mei in the flesh at a combination Arby's/gas station in Greenville, S.C. There's something about the smell of roast beef and high octane that to this day makes me wistfully sentimental.

Mei's "cousin-sister," Susan, a dynamic corporate executive who came to America at the age of 14 with nothing and forged a very successful life for herself, was our chaperone. Her husband and one-time email helper, George, a doctor by trade (well, a podiatrist ... with all due respect, the guy handles *feet*) smartly stayed home. But their one-year-old son, Reid, joined us.

I arrived at Arby's first and sat in a booth close to the door so I could spy ... er, watch out for them. They pulled up in Susan's car, stepped out, and went to the trunk to get a stroller for Reid. It was easy to tell them apart because I knew Mei wasn't the driver. I first noticed her long black hair, olive skin, and cute shape. I'd like to be able to say something about her clothes, but I don't remember. I'm a guy.

Susan looked pretty nice herself. I was about to have lunch with two attractive Chinese women. That just doesn't happen to me often. I didn't realize at the time that sharing meals with Chinese people would soon become a running theme in my life.

I thought about walking out to meet them, but I didn't want to appear too eager. So I stayed inside as they slowly approached. I greeted them as soon as they walked in, and we went to a booth near the back of the restaurant.

Mei didn't say much — writing English was easier for her than speaking it, at that time — and she appeared subservient to Susan.

Mei and I sat on one side of the booth as I faced Susan on the other side. I was relaxed. Xanax will do that for you. I broke the ice by joking that I was a fit suitor for Mei because I seldom drool in public, I don't own a monkey, and I no longer sell burned-out light bulbs to blind people.

Susan laughed, but then the grilling began, and I don't mean just in the kitchen. I answered all of her questions — and her, mine — to our mutual satisfaction and the conversation breezed along.

"So I hear you work for a newspaper," Susan said. "Are you going to write about this meeting?"

"No, I promise I will never write about this," I replied. I meant it at the time.

Little Reid was very cute, and they could tell I was good with children. The problem was, I was only good with them for a limited period of time. When I got tired of them, which was quickly, I could always hand them off to the parents and go back to the peace and quiet of my own abode. If this first date would ever lead to children, I wondered how I would handle it.

I learned that "Susan" was not her real name. She's called Susan to "Americanize" her and to give her an easy name to pronounce. A lot of Chinese people do this when they come to America. But they don't always pick the best names. Susan is okay, but some of her Chinese friends, such as Daphne and Fanny, just seemed to pick names out of the phonebook without knowing whether or not they are old-fashioned or cool.

Meanwhile, I cut my eyes over to Mei to see if she was still breathing. But her appearance and demeanor didn't click with me until Susan got up to take Reid to the bathroom to change him. I then took the opportunity to lean over and gave Mei a sly smile and a little "hi." She tilted her head and hunched her shoulders and burst out with an embarrassing grin, the kind of thing a little girl would do after she got caught with her hand in the cookie jar. In that sweet moment of shyness, I saw her dimples and realized she was the girl for me. I loved Mei's mind and soul before I met her. Now I could see that she was physically attractive to me as well. This was a far cry from that Van Klumpp woman.

Susan returned with Reid, and as she sat back down, she handed me this bombshell: "Fred, you have to understand that there is to be no sex before marriage. That is something we do not do in our country."

"Oh, that's fine with me," I lied. I wasn't too keen on that until I remembered my friend Eddie, who had sex with his first wife before he was married to her, but none after. So I thought this might be a better deal.

And that was the extent of our date. We all shook hands and parted company.

Not knowing how they really felt about me, I pondered the lunch during my long drive home. All kinds of emotions ran through me. I felt anxious. I felt apprehensive. And, for about ten seconds, I felt Amish. I don't know where that came from but suddenly I forgot how to drive the "strange machine" I was in and almost wrecked.

I knew that when I walked through the door of my house and turned on the computer, I would receive either a thumbs up or down from Mei.

FOUR
GETTING ORIENTED

In Mei's email, she thanked me for coming to Greenville and said she enjoyed meeting me. She went on to say she liked my green eyes and had a "first sight attraction." Apparently, she and Susan liked me very much, and Mei had a "special feeling" about me.

Yeah!

No doubt I was relieved. I e-mailed her back and told her I was equally impressed. Then I watched some sexy Japanimation to bone up.

I stayed awake in bed, very excited. I was getting the feeling that I was on the doorstep of some great adventure. Either that, or I'd have to change my name and move out of the country. Regardless, it was better than sitting around the house watching the milk in my refrigerator expire.

More e-mails followed. The distance between us made it difficult to get to know her better by taking her out to a few movies and dinners. Each occasion had to be planned to get the most out of it.

We set up another meeting two weeks after our first one. Only this time I would be staying overnight at the apartment Mei shared with Susan, Reid, and George in Greenville. I worried about my panic attacks and wondered if the medication would keep them under control.

This was the big one. If I messed it up, our future together could be in jeopardy.

It started out fine. I arrived early on a Saturday afternoon, overnight bag in hand. Mei greeted me at the door, and she looked great. I watched her as she moved about the apartment. It seemed as though she was floating. She was very graceful and elegant.

It struck me during my visit that it was filled with clichès: We took our shoes off, we ate rice (the Chinese eat it for virtually every meal, with nothing on it, and gummy so that it can be picked up with chopsticks), we played karaoke and Chinese checkers (no kidding!), and we watched "The Joy Luck Club" on video. Boy! I was immersed in Chinese culture head to toe.

Mei was at once cook, maid, and baby sitter. Obviously, she was a hard worker. And the meal she prepared was scrumptious, true Chinese cuisine, not like the stuff you get in the restaurants.

Unfortunately, I picked up some tofu thinking it was chicken. I am not a gourmet. I'm a meat-and-potatoes guy with a few carrots, beans, and some corn on the cob thrown in. "Exotic" foods like tofu (*toe-phooey* I call it) are not my thing. But once it was in my mouth, I couldn't very well spit it out with Mei and Susan looking at me. I forced myself to swallow it along the rest of the tofu I mistakenly put on my plate. This put a permanent end to my relationship with tofu.

Through observing what was going on and what was said, I learned that it's the *women* who run the household. This has been borne out in every Chinese-American home I've seen since. In fact, the phrase "yes, dear" was invented by American men married to Chinese women.

But I still maintained a fantasy notion that my wife would run my bath water and give me a massage every night before we went to bed. I was in for a cultural awakening!

Mei and I took a walk to a nearby park and attempted a conversation. It was difficult at first. She was not nearly so good with my language as in her e-mails, without the benefit of a dictionary or Susan at her side. I would say something like, "I love the NFL" (my favorite thing in the world), and she would reply, in perfect English, "Huh?"

I thought it would be good to talk about something we were both familiar with. So I asked, "What do you think of Charlie Chan?"

She said, "Oh, yes, I think he's great. Jackie Chan is just great."

"Er, that Confucius was a pretty smart fellow," I continued.

"Who?" she asked.

"Confucius. Isn't he Chinese? He's famous in the West," I said.

She didn't know about whom I was speaking. Apparently, Confucius goes by a different name over there.

It was not the most normal of conversations. But I took some pratfalls on the park grounds to put Mei at ease, and she laughed easily at my attempts at physical humor. That meant a lot to me. I had the feeling that in time we would be okay.

That night something happened that would "seal the deal" between Mei and me. We were invited to a party given by one of Susan's friends. After we went through the buffet, we found ourselves alone in the living room, and we seized the moment for our first kiss. It was magic. Mei, confidently and in the most exquisite English I've ever heard, said, "You make me feel like a woman." That was just what I needed to hear. I would have kissed her more, but I had too much potato salad in my mouth.

For the rest of the party, we held each other. The feelings that were so close to the surface, the feelings for which we dared not hope, bubbled over. We were in love!

But come Sunday morning, with sunshine in my face and the liquor out of my system, I began to get what we men like to call "cold feet" (maybe this was a case for Susan's podiatrist husband). I started feeling anxious. This was due in part to the medication I was on. Frankly, I took too much of it Saturday to get me through the ordeal. And I was coming down hard.

Mei and I went shopping Sunday afternoon, and at the mall she did something that I'll always remember. She wore a necklace with a small locket and key, and she held them and said to me, "Will you let me unlock the key to your heart?" Then I —

Mr. Grumpy — in a sarcastic tone, said, "Well, my heart has a combination lock." Ha, ha. Very funny!

We kissed some more, but that's as far as it went. I wanted to touch her body, but she made it clear to me that wasn't going to happen. Really, I was content just to get out of there and head home.

My age at the time, forty-two, belied my sexual experience. Because panic attacks took me out of action through my late teens and early adult life, I was more of a Don Knotts than a Don Juan in the romance department.

I thought about what I wanted all night during the drive home. What I wanted, I said to myself, was assurance from Mei in the sex department. After I got home, in the nicest and stupidest way possible, I e-mailed her and asked what I was to expect sexually. If we couldn't make love before we were married, how was I supposed to know we'd be sexually compatible after we got married?

This was not what Mei wanted to hear. She fired back that she was shocked and offended. She said if I was looking for someone who I could touch all over on the first date, I should pay someone. She added that if she did what I wanted, she might not respect me or herself.

She wanted me to know that Chinese women are "not as stupid as you think." She said Chinese women know sex just like American women do, but one thing is different: Chinese women respect men and themselves more than American women do.

It hit me hard when she ended the e-mail saying she felt "confused, useless, and naive." But she thought I was a nice man who has doubts, and if we couldn't find happiness with each other, she was glad we met.

Yikes! Needless to say, I goofed. It turned out Mei was a woman of high character. Drat! No, I'm kidding; I couldn't have asked for a better person with whom to share my life (and comics).

All I could do was e-mail her back and tell her I was sorry. This was the first of many, many, many apologies to Mei. I told her I certainly didn't think she was stupid, and I did not mean to give the impression I wanted to have sex with her that weekend. I just had questions about our future and now she had answered them.

I also wrote that I wanted her to make me a better man. Now keep in mind this was six months before Jack Nicholson said it in "As Good As It Gets." A lawsuit is pending.

I didn't hear back from Mei for a day. I remember cutting the grass the next evening and thinking about how I screwed up my life again. I finished the lawn and went inside to see if I had received any e-mails from her. I had.

Everything was okay. Two of Mei's gifts are patience and tolerance. Yes, she was a good catch. But so was I, and she knew it. She wanted to give the relationship every chance. I'm glad she did.

About a week later, on June 6 (the D-Day anniversary, wouldn't you know?) after some very special e-mails, I called her and asked her to marry me. She said "yes," and we were both overjoyed. But we had no frame of reference for what to expect next.

FIVE
RULES OF ENGAGEMENT

There's a little known loophole in the before-marriage contract between consenting adults in China. After they're engaged, a couple is allowed to have sex, with the blessing of the family. It's the "try-out period," so that both the man and the woman know what to fully expect in the bedroom.

So Susan was conning me, I thought. *There is sex before marriage after all*. I was ecstatic about it!

We arranged our first encounter for my next trip to Greenville. Here's where the chain of events gets strange. Susan helped Mei and me get a hotel room, and she escorted us to the door. We went inside, both so scared that we briefly took up smoking. Susan closed the door and left the hotel, knowing full well what her little cousin was going to be doing sometime over the next several hours. Once home, Susan patiently awaited the "test results." Talk about performance anxiety!

Neither one of us knew what to do at that moment. I had brought a bottle of champagne, and we both took a few nervous sips. Since we were barely at the talking stage at this point, with Mei's spoken English still broken and slow, I decided actions speak louder than words. I made sure she wasn't wearing a chastity belt and jumped right in.

Without getting too graphic, I can best describe the action by using a football metaphor: After a penalty due to a false start, I fumbled, had my backfield in motion and got sacked. But eventually I intercepted a pass and penetrated her territory. I then plowed through an opening near her own end zone and scored. But I did not spike the ball.

I quickly discovered that I needn't have worried about a satisfying sexual life. Mei was every inch a woman. And I was every inch a man ... there just weren't that many inches involved.

I also found out a most interesting aspect about Mei's body: She had no hair on her legs. They were not only shapely, but also smooth. *Hubba, hubba!*

Mei loved my gentle touch. She was astounded that my hands were so soft. There was no need to tell her that they were the result of avoiding physical labor for years.

Later in our hotel room, I got my first real chance

to talk with Mei for an extended period. She told me of her life in China, how she loved her homeland and how much she missed her family, and especially her daughter, Dan Dan. She wept when she recalled how homesick she had been.

This was a proud, sensitive woman; she was very soft-spoken and genuine. I was convinced I had made the right choice.

She also made me aware of my enormous responsibility: She was an immigrant. She had no job. She had no Social Security number. She could not drive. Her daughter was still in China, and we would have to work through Immigration to get her out.

But I was ready for the challenge. Up until that moment I had basically lived just for me. I passed the hours fighting boredom without making any real difference in people's lives. Now I was able to help someone, which gave my life a sense of purpose. Besides, I could truthfully say I had nothing better to do.

The next morning we left the hotel and went back to Susan's apartment. Careful glances between the two of them let me know I was "in."

Now it was Mei's turn to visit my home and find

out what it's really like to live in America, or at least in Goose Creek, South Carolina, which is about the same.

I told my mom to prepare for a weekend visitor. She was not too happy about the prospect, but I reassured her that Mei was not at all like my last girlfriend, Princess Quadilladilla (not her real name), who was somewhat loud and sassy and packed a rod. I told her Mei was quiet, respectful, and sweet, and she had never discharged a firearm. I knew Mom would fall in love with her as easily as I did.

"Well, we'll see," Mom said, adding, "now go buy me some teeth."

SIX
THE VISIT

An e-mail to Mei from me on June 15:

Mei, I love you.

Some people may not find an e-mail love letter very romantic. But isn't an e-mail every bit as valid as a paper love letter, as long as what is written is sincere and from the heart?

Imagine our difficulties if there was no Internet, and all of our letters had to be hand-written and mailed? By this time we would not even be past the introduction phase.

I eagerly await your arrival, though it is still some days away. I'm very excited.

Please be relaxed when you come to visit. I don't want to push you; I don't want to spoil our romantic adventure. We'll take it easy. I'll play you some movies, we'll ride bikes, we'll visit my best friend, Mark, we'll tour Charleston, and I'll show you the ocean.

The weekend we shared our first kiss, I still had my "wall" up, my mental barrier that prevents me from getting too close and allows me to turn away from change and challenge. But now I have torn down that wall, for you, and all barriers to my heart. You have conquered me.

Mei replied that she couldn't sleep nights and had to take sleeping pills. But that she would be okay once she saw me again, on Friday, as we planned to go to city court in Greenville to get our marriage license.

So I went to Greenville to get the license and bring Mei back to Goose Creek for the weekend.

Let me give you a little description of the scenery on I-26 through South Carolina. One word: flat. No mountains. No valleys. No lakes. No volcanoes. Just lots of trees and a lot of farmland, especially from the mid-state down to Charleston. The area is called the Lowcountry for that reason.

So it's pretty boring. And since you can't get off on the sights, you have to entertain yourself in other ways, like through stimulating conversation. But we didn't talk much at all. We almost needed a translator, because Mei still had a long way to go with her spoken English.

However, the drive still was pleasant, because this was one of the few trips on which I did *not* have to listen to a woman yakkin' at me the whole way. My last girlfriend talked incessantly. The problem was not so much a woman talking — it was having to listen and respond in an appropriate and timely fashion, a crucial skill during the dating period.

Mei is one of the few women I've known who believes silence is golden. Again, I knew she was the woman for me.

Instead of gabbing, I played a cassette of my favorite songs, everything from CCR to Sinatra to Alice Cooper to the Beatles (I know, I'm old). This was the language we spoke, the language of music. I did kid her about John Lennon's enigmatic lyric "Goo goo goo ga joob" from "I Am a Walrus." I told her it was a very common American expression, and I was surprised she didn't know it.

All joking aside, I had a confession to make to her: In some of my e-mails, I "cheated." On at least two occasions, I used lyrics from songs as if I made them up. I remember using "I need you more than want you, and I want you for all time" from Glen Campbell's "Wichita Lineman," with credit to Jimmy Webb's lyric. But then that song came up on the cassette, so I thought it best to 'fess up.

We pulled up into my driveway. I didn't know it,

but this was the first in a series of disappointments for Mei.

False notion No. 1: Mei will be impressed with my house.

Wrong. Though Mei had never lived in a house with a yard, she had visited the homes of her Chinese friends in Greenville. They were much newer and larger than mine. Basically, I lived in a 1,000-square-foot brick box, with one bathroom. It was good enough for my mom and me, but not for Mei. But she didn't say anything, and in my blissful ignorance, I thought *she* thought I lived like a *king*.

False notion No. 2: Mei will love living in my neighborhood.

Wrong. It was an older neighborhood, by now lower-middle class, and while it wasn't a bad neighborhood at the time, it was not what she had hoped.

False notion No. 3: Mei won't mind Droopy, my Basset hound.

Wrong. Droopy was totally neurotic and hard for anyone to love. She barked, whined, demanded my attention, and acted like a spoiled child. At about four o'clock nearly every morning she would come to my bedroom door and whine until I got up and calmed her down.

This appalled Mei. No one in China ever carried on so much about a dog. In fact, they *eat* dogs over there. Perhaps to Mei, it was like having a pig in the house. Also, though I didn't realize it, Mei told me Droopy was a stinkpot.

On the plus side, Mei met my mom, and the two got along great. Mark, my best friend, came over with his future wife, Janice, and they wished us luck. Mark called me as soon as he got home and said, "Fred, I'm impressed!"

I played Mei some of my favorite movies on Friday night — films that practically every American has seen, but they were all new to her: "Jaws" (after it was over, she exclaimed in her cute way, "That's the best movie I never saw!"); "A Hard Day's Night" with the Beatles; and "It's a Mad Mad Mad Mad World," a classic slapstick comedy. Mei had a problem with a lot of the dialogue ("You Americans talk so fast!"), but she appreciated those particular films for their visuals, music, and physical comedy.

I also played Mei a Three Stooges episode, "Cactus Makes Perfect" — a true classic. This was important because if she didn't like it, it would mean we didn't share the same sense of humor. Well, I was relieved to find out Mei loved the Stooges. I wasn't laughing at them anymore because I had seen the episodes so many times. But I got a fresh kick watching Mei enjoy them.

Saturday morning we strolled around downtown Charleston and took in the historic Market area, with its myriad of dealers selling everything from ceramics to copper. To my surprise, Mei didn't buy anything, though I told her to spend my money freely. Later at Northwoods Mall, she bought me a watch, with *her* money. *Hey, this is a gal I can afford to live with!* I thought.

We went to the Isle of Palms, a local beach, though I had to buy her a swimsuit. I started to get her a thong and make her wear it backwards, but I thought better of it.

Even though Mei adored her first view of the ocean, the beach was not her thing. She couldn't swim (neither could I, I'm ashamed to admit), and she wasn't used to the powerful waves and eye-stinging salt water.

At a sandwich shop on the strip, I bought her a chili dog, handed it to her, and she sort of just stared at it. I didn't realize it was her first one until she asked, "Uh, which way to eat this, from the side or the ends?"

Saturday night we drank champagne and made love. Sunday morning we rode bicycles through the neighborhood, but the stifling summer heat drove us indoors. Mei was not used to the humidity in Charleston. As a matter of fact, nobody ever gets used to it.

By the second day, Mom had fallen in love with Mei, as everyone does, and she was happy that at last she was going to have a daughter-in-law. Though her mental capabilities were flagging, it turned out to be somewhat of a blessing because Mom used simple words and phrases and Mei was able to understand her.

Susan and George drove down to pick up Mei late Sunday afternoon. George seemed to like my collection of vintage comic books and my "Lost in Space" robot model (could it be that Ezmirelda Van Klumpp was right, that I was still that nine-year-old boy, perpetually frozen in time in 1964? Naaahhh!). They didn't stay long. I kissed Mei goodbye and told her the next time we met would be our wedding day, which was set for June 28. I was sure they had a lot to talk about on the way home. I thought they were singing my praises. Boy, I was wrong.

SEVEN
THE REACTION

My friends and family, along with my co-workers at *The Post and Courier*, were at once puzzled, fascinated, and sickened by this sudden romance. Reaction was not mixed. They were *all* skeptical. And some were waiting for me to fall on my face.

Frank Wooten, an editorial writer for the paper and a very witty fellow, was initially suspicious. He warned me: "Fred, don't you get it? You're forty-two years old. You're short. You're not rich. *She's a spy!*"

Another co-worker quipped, "Maybe she's an *old* digger!"

Janice, Mark's future wife, sounded a warning that proved prophetic. She said, "Fred, before you know it, she's gonna have her mamma, her daddy, and her brothers all living with you!" (She must have been psychic! But more on that later.)

My sister, Cindy, and my brother, Jeff, both younger than me, called from Cincinnati and Seattle respectively, and neither knew what to think. My sister and I were never close (that would change, which I'll explain later); she didn't even know about my panic attacks. To her, I was this weird, self-centered nerd who didn't know how to enjoy life. My sister's idea of enjoying life, at least in the old days, was sex, drugs, and rock 'n' roll. And the older I get, the more I realize she was probably right.

I was closer to my brother, but I hadn't seen him in three years. He had his own demons with which to contend, but he still wished me luck.

Only two people were straight-forward and brave enough to tell me I was nuts: Barbara Williams, then-executive editor at the paper, and my boss at the time, Margaret Garrett.

"Fred, don't do this," Margaret said in a tone akin to a mother scolding a child. I was certainly not angry with her for saying that. In fact, I appreciated her concern. I simply told both Barbara and Margaret: "If you spend just five minutes with this girl, you will understand."

Margaret promised not to fire me for being a lamebrain until after she met Mei and checked her out. As my boss, Margaret was never very sure about me. She told others she couldn't figure me out. I couldn't figure her out, either. Frankly, I thought Margaret's posterior was a bit tight. In retrospect, she was strange to me because she possessed something I had seldom seen: class.

But I continued to give her fits. One morning I came in, late as usual, and she said, "Fred, you've been coming in late and leaving early."

My reply: "That's my style!" It was such a good comeback that she couldn't get mad at me.

One time during an evaluation of my work she told me I needed to "push the envelope" a little. The next day she saw me on the street corner selling stationery.

Okay, I'm kidding. But she had legitimate concerns. Why did I ask Mei to marry me so soon? What's the rush? This was my answer: When I see what I want, I go after it (and every seventeenth time, I get it!). I wanted to scoop Mei up before any of those *other* sexual deviants on the Web got their hands on her.

Also, it just wasn't practical continuing a long-distance love affair. The only way to see Mei every day was to marry her. And besides, think of the gas it would save!

EIGHT
NO RICE AT THE WEDDING?

The long-distance phase of our romance came to an end on Saturday, June 28, 1997, when I arrived in Greenville to get Mei.

Our wedding was scheduled for five o'clock at my grandmother's house in North Charleston. Mei's dreams of a huge American-style wedding with gowns and cakes and bridesmaids and churches were not to be. First, she didn't express those wishes to me until after we were married. Second, I just didn't have the dough, not even for a cake.

It rained practically all the way from Greenville to Charleston. By the time we splashed our way through a flooded Northwoods Mall parking lot to buy the rings, it was 4 p.m.

We stopped at KFC to buy food for the "reception." I said, "Hey, Mei, get a load of this: boxed chicken. I bet you've never seen anything like this!" Little did I know there are about a million KFCs in China. We arrived at my grandmother's house about ten minutes before show time.

The guest list consisted of my grandmother; my mother; Mark and Janice; and two co-workers, Ellen (my code breaker on that hideous night in Savannah) and Emily Abedon. I informed Mei that Emily and Ellen were my ex-girlfriends. They weren't. But it didn't hurt to have her believe that.

Christine Randall, a co-worker, Notary and "ex-girlfriend," performed the ceremony. At first she wanted us to read out loud to each other some romantic stuff she found in a book. I pulled her aside and explained, "Look, Mei is going to have a hard enough time just repeating the regular wedding vows. I don't want to embarrass her." Christine agreed.

My Uncle Henry, who lived in the house with my grandmother (*his mother* — do you sense a trend in our family?), was not mysteriously absent, just absent. There was no mystery about it: This was a guy who got mad at me for buying a Toyota instead of an American car. So I could imagine his indignation, not only at my marrying a Chinese woman but possibly not even trading her in after four years.

As the rain continued to pour, Mei and I exchanged vows, slipped rings on our fingers and were officially man and wife. Then the guests ate fried chicken. Crispy, not regular.

So this was our big wedding. It may not have been romantic, but it counted!

Mei and I then drove to the Woodlands, a very fine (i.e. incredibly expensive) restaurant and inn in the small, pastoral town of Summerville. During dinner, while talking about our future, I started feeling a bit queasy. The old panic attack syndrome was rearing its ugly head, cutting through the medication. I went to the restroom to compose myself. I was all right. It was just the normal wedding day jitters that any groom might feel.

I splashed water on my face and looked at myself in the mirror. *Hey, Dad,* I thought, *Look at me now. I made it.*

Though he made mistakes and had more than his share of problems, and even though he was surely disappointed in me at times, my father always loved me. And he would have been proud this day.

But as I continued to gaze in the mirror, I had to ask myself a question: *So, what happens now?*

I had cleverly arranged for my mom to stay with my grandmother through the weekend, so Mei and I had the house all to ourselves. I carried — or attempted to carry — Mei over the threshold for our wedding night. This is how I got my hiatal hernia, and it's all Mei's fault! If she hadn't eaten that heavy dessert at the Woodlands, I might have managed the task without injury.

But we were in such haste to get married that we didn't look at the calendar closely enough. This was not an ideal time of the month for Mei.

Oh well, I learned early what most husbands have already found out, marriage isn't really about the sex.

NINE
'OPEN THE LIGHT'

"Fred, marriage changes you," George told me shortly after the wedding.

I didn't believe him at the time. I thought I was too set in my ways. I also felt that, since Mei was coming out of a bad marriage, I wouldn't really have to try all that hard, as long as I was better than what she had before.

How stupid can a man be?

The morning after the wedding, I awoke to Mei cleaning the blades of my window fan. Right away I knew my world would be tidier, if nothing else. She also shined several pairs of shoes that had never seen polish in their long lives.

The first Friday evening after we married, I did what I always did: I went to Mark's house. I had been going to Mark's house very Friday night for twelve years. That wasn't going to change, in my view. Of course, I took Mei with me. It would be her last visit there.

Mei had seen some strange cultural rituals, but

nothing like this. We crowded into Mark's extremely small, windowless den with Janice and her two granddaughters. Having known me since they were infants, the granddaughters, now pre-teens, wanted to see this multicultural union up close and personal. But we didn't just talk. Mark set up a projector, and we all watched a 16 mm film. That's right, a film, a strip of pictures with holes in it, which fit through sprockets onto a pickup reel, and runs past a light which projected the pictures onto a movie screen. How old school can you get?

But Mark didn't show home movies. That would be bad enough. No, he showed, with my blessing, an old Japanese Ultra-Man TV episode from 1967. Why? Because both Mark and I collected old 16 mm films at the time. We're geeks, remember? Worse: We're retro-geeks.

So here's Mei, in a strange room, in a strange land, with strange people watching a strange Japanese picture show! Not even Chinese! When the twenty-five minute reel ended, I looked at Mei. She said nothing. I said, "Do you want to go home?" She said, "Yes, please." I went to Mark's house the following Friday. Alone.

We eventually took a short honeymoon to Myrtle Beach, about a two-hour drive away. I only had a few days off from work because I had taken a lot of vacation time courting Mei.

Myrtle Beach is not very romantic. In fact, it has crass commercialism written all over it, but that didn't bother Mei. She wasn't used to seeing a million billboards, miniature golf courses, and neon signs all crowded into a few miles. To her, it was unusual, lively, and fun.

Not long after our Myrtle Beach excursion, I got home from work one evening and asked Mei if she wanted to go to the drugstore with me. No big deal, right? But she got all dressed up in a fantastic Chinese jade gown, looking like she was about to attend a formal dinner. I said, "Mei, we're going to an Eckerds in Goose Creek, South Carolina. It's not the Taj Mahal."

But that was Mei's style. She always looked her best. The first month I watched her intently as she went to work around the house. She bought new curtains and bedspreads. She introduced each new element slowly, instinctively knowing that too many changes too quickly would make me uncomfortable.

For my part, I helped Mei along with her English,

making sure she learned all the major curse words. Her English improved, but she still had trouble pronouncing certain words, and her voice inflections were a bit off. One evening I saw her cooking something in the frying pan. I asked her what it was. She said "tofu" but it sounded like "dog food."

Puzzled, I asked, "You're cooking it?"

"Sure," she replied. "You want some?"

"Er, no thanks," I said. "But Droopy will be delighted."

Then it hit me what she meant.

This kind of dialogue was not uncommon. Here are our Top Ten classic communication crack-ups that actually took place:

1) I was talking *shoes*. Mei, still learning basic English in the fall of '97, for one silly moment mistook the word "shoe" to mean "bra."

I said: "You know Christine, the woman I work with who married us? She must have 100 pairs of shoes."

"Really? Why?" Mei asked, thinking "bras."

"I dunno. She likes to show them off at work, I guess. You know. Flats. Pumps. Black. Red. She paid 200 dollars for one pair."

Mei, now totally bewildered, could only ask, "*Why*

would she pay 200 dollars for a *shoe*?"

Then I realized what was happening.

I asked: "Do you know what I'm talking about?"

Mei put both hands up to her chest and made a crossing motion.

"Nooooo!" I pointed down at my feet. "Shoes! Not bras!"

2) When we saw a news report about tornadoes in the Midwest, she asked, "Do you think *tomatoes* will come here?"

"Oh, yeah," I replied. "Bunches of them!"

3) A friend of Mei's was in the hospital having surgery. I asked her what the trouble was.

"She has a problem with her, uh, what do you call them?" She pointed to her stomach area. "You have two of them…."

"Oh, kidneys," I replied.

She said, "Yes, her o'kidneys."

4) Mei called me at work to tell me that the appliance repairman had "left a stove."

I said, "He left a stove? We have two stoves?"

She said we had five of them. She was referring to the burners.

5) I asked Mei if she had ever heard of Shirley Temple.

"Yes," she replied. "I've been there."

She thought I was talking about the Shaolin Temple.

6) Mei pronounced ice as "ass." One night I asked her if she needed anything from the store while I was there, and she told me to buy her some "ass cream." Not wanting to know the details, I came back with a tube of Preparation H.

7) I bought Mei a VCR, and she said she wanted to pay me back.

I said, "No, that's okay. I don't want you to owe me."

Mei mistook the word "owe" for "own." She didn't speak to me for several hours after that.

8) My responsibilities at the newspaper shifted from writing and editing to page designing. But whenever someone would ask Mei what I did for a living, she would say, "He's a page desire."

9) When Mei got a job at a Chinese restaurant she had to learn such basic words as "straw" and "napkin." Early on, a customer asked if she had any bread. Mei's answer: "No, this is a Chinese restaurant. No breast."

10) And when a couple walked in to ask about the price of the buffet, Mei answered, "Lunch is $4.99.

With drink and sex, $5.99." Of course she meant to say *tax*.

I'm never surprised at how much Mei knows and doesn't know about the English language. For example, she learned the word "metaphor" early in the marriage, but after five years, she still didn't know the word "while." She had heard me say it countless times, but never bothered to ask me what the hell it meant.

And some of her expressions were so cute that I didn't correct her. Throughout our marriage, she referred to "turn on the light" as "open the light." And she always "washed" her teeth.

Back to the topic of Mei's cooking: She was great at Chinese dishes but had a lot to learn in the culinary ways of the West. For example, she boiled a roast on the stove because she didn't know how to use an oven. When Mei was growing up, most Chinese homes did not have ovens. As a result, the Chinese are not big on things like casseroles, baked ham, pies, or cakes.

Mei slowly learned to cook some of the things I liked, but as a neophyte not only in the preparation of the meal but also to the actual taste, she never knew if she messed anything up unless I told her.

This would lead to the inevitable comment, "Well, if you don't like it why don't you try cooking it yourself?" I did try, and after a few botched attempts, I realized I was better off sticking with Mei's cooking, good or bad. My biggest complaint about cooking is that it takes hours to do it and clean up afterward, but only five minutes to eat it.

We watched at least one movie a night at home as Mei began to appreciate American cinema, though of course American films had been showing in China for decades. We also went out to the movies. Often Mei didn't know what was happening in the films. She would whisper to me, "What's going on?" I would usually keep my answers simple and to the point: "Uh, she hates him."

I took Mei to the newspaper office and introduced her to the gang. Everyone, including my boss, Margaret, took an instant liking to her. I was not fired.

I don't know how, but Mei somehow got the idea that I was the publisher. It must have been one of those little "misunderstandings." After I brought her in, I immediately started ordering everyone around. Mei wondered, if I was the "boss," why did my "employees" tell me to shut up and go "F" myself?

I also introduced Mei to the classic American sit-com, "I Love Lucy." After one episode — a favorite of mine in which Lucy meets William Holden, dumps a whole tray of food on him in a restaurant and later has to wear a fake nose when Ricky brings Holden home to meet her — Mei was hooked. It felt neat to pass on this legacy of classic comedy from a half-century ago to a Chinese woman who had never heard of it. In another typical "Mei-ism," she referred to Fred and Ethel on the show as "Fred and Awful."

When it came to restaurants, I started Mei out slowly, then we worked our way up the food chain. First, the Waffle House (so, what's wrong with waffles? Mei had never eaten them before), then Shoney's, then Applebee's, then Olive Garden, and on to some of the fine Charleston eateries. One of the reasons Charleston is a world-class tourist destination is the restaurant fare. "Charleston has some of the finest restaurants in the world," said Peter Falk when he filmed a "Columbo" episode at The Citadel, South Carolina's military college, many moons ago. Falk has since passed, but I know it wasn't from our food.

Mei truly loved American cuisine, but Chinese food remains her favorite.

Mei was born with the shopping gene and could stay in Wal-Mart for hours. I like Wal-Mart too. It's one of the few stores where you can buy meat and pants. And on the subject of pants, Mei declared she hated my clothes (maybe she was allergic to polyester) and set out to buy me a new wardrobe. She redid me from head to toe, and I must say I did look better — if not GQ.

I thought I would have a problem getting Mei interested in the National Football League, but she liked the sport from the get-go. She caught on to the nuances of the game. She appreciated the art of a toe-tapping sideline catch as well as the power of a running back blasting through a defensive line.

She got to know the players and coaches, especially the handsome ones like quarterback Steve Young, then of San Francisco, and head coach John Gruden, then of Oakland.

During the '97 season she watched at least part of almost every game with me. She even accompanied me to sports bars to watch some of the games that weren't shown in our area. I later got a satellite dish to remedy that situation.

But she was so new to the game that just about

any simple play excited her. If a quarterback threw a five-yard swing pass to a tight end, she'd exclaim, "Wow! What a play!"

I enjoyed having her company so much that '97 turned out to be my favorite NFL season. As time went on, Mei gradually lost much of her initial interest in the game. Still, I cherished those times when she would take a moment to sit down with me and watch an exciting scoring drive.

Mei made frequent calls to China to talk with her daughter Dan Dan, her mother, and her three brothers. Her family, in turn, made numerous calls to us, but often the calls came in the middle of the night. There is a twelve-hour time difference between the East Coast and Mei's hometown of Jilin City, or 13 hours depending on Daylight Savings Time. So we'd get calls at 3 a.m.

Did her family members know about the time difference? Of course they did. But they called anyway! The funny thing about some Chinese people is that when they have something to tell you, it doesn't bother them if they wake you up to tell you. If they have some kind of problem, it has to be solved *now*!

We received quite a few of these early-morning

calls until I had to put my foot down and make Mei tell them to stop the insanity.

My wife continued to amaze me every day. She was a natural at sports. Having never picked up a baseball or swung a bat, she could throw and hit like a guy, though she had a problem with bowling. On her first attempt, she threw the ball behind her.

Mei loved to dance, too, but her ex-husband had forbidden her to do it. She even won a dance contest on local Chinese television. But instead of her husband being proud of her, he smashed her trophy on the floor. He never wanted Mei to get attention or have any friends.

On the other hand, I really enjoyed watching Mei gracefully glide across the living room, dancing to the music on my stereo. I don't like to dance myself, unless I am very intoxicated, and even then I only do the "Hokey Pokey."

A few months into the marriage, as I watched Mei dance and smile, something struck me: *I really loved this woman*! I thought I loved her before, but I didn't even know what love was until this, the real thing, came along.

Indeed, Mei, too, was in love. And she liked being able to express herself. "You give me freedom," she said. I told her I didn't *give* her freedom. Freedom was already hers…except when it came to the remote control!

But Mei was still homesick. She often cried while looking at photos of her family. She worried about working through Immigration to get her daughter to America. And, frankly, she was bored. She couldn't drive or work yet. So she spent her days sitting around the house watching *Jerry Springer* and thinking those nuts on his show were average Americans. (I had to tell the truth: They *were*!)

Was this the best that life in the States had to offer?

TEN
I PUT MEI ON A FAST PLANE TO CHINA, BUT WILL SHE RETURN TO ME?

Mei received a call from China in the fall of '97. Usually, I was not able to ascertain what her phone conversations were all about, but I was certainly able to sense fear and worry in her voice this time. Her father was sick, and she wanted to see him and the rest of her family. Of course, I didn't protest. Mei desperately missed her daughter, and we realized it might take *years* to get her to America. That's the way it works with Immigration. And this was before 9/11.

The next day I watched Mei, accompanied by Susan, walk to the plane for her supposed two-week stay in China. I wasn't 100 percent sure she would come back. Maybe America wasn't as great as she thought it was. Maybe I wasn't as great as she thought I was.

Meanwhile, this was my chance to enjoy bachelor-hood again. It was just like old times: I was burping, farting, and renting porn tapes. But this time it was kind of empty. Hard to believe, I know.

Mei and I spoke to each other on the phone nearly every day. Her father's health was improving, and she was enjoying her trip, visiting old friends who threw parties for her. Mei was extremely popular in her hometown, Jilin City. She was the talk of her circle of friends. Their little Mei was married to an American. Everyone was interested. They had questions. Such as, is it true Americans actually pull thread between their teeth after brushing?

I counted the days until her return. On October 17, I drove to Greenville to George's apartment to meet Mei, who was landing in Atlanta and coming to Greenville by car with Susan. Well, the plane was delayed. Not only that, George wasn't even home. So I spent the night at a hotel.

The next day, the 18th, was the ten-year anniversary of my first dental surgery. Back then my teeth and gums were in pretty bad shape. I never had braces but should have, my wisdom teeth came in late, I had abscesses, and my gums were receding and bleeding. Not a pretty picture, but because of my panic attacks, I feared the dental chair. Once I conquered the attacks, it was still hard to face the dentist, with all the problems that had developed.

They had only gotten worse because I delayed fixing them. But I finally went through it all.

The periodontist told me I had a pocket in my gums big enough to put small change in, and I had to have skin scraped off the roof of my mouth to make a graft to plug it up. I also had to have nine teeth pulled in one day so I could get three bridges installed (as well as two overpasses and a tunnel).

I had come a long way in the decade, and even with all the roadwork in my mouth, I felt triumphant as I watched Mei and Susan finally arrive.

Mei's return affected me in a profound way. She gave up China for me! I wanted to yell, "I'm not worthy!" I knew I would somehow have to become worthy.

After Mei came home, she showed me a home video of herself and her family in China. It really got to me when I watched her and her three brothers — all handsome, well-dressed young adults — stand in historic Tianamen Square in Beijing, and in English her oldest brother said, "Fred, welcome to family, welcome to China."

Wow! That put a lump in my throat. Up until

that time, I was hesitant about going to China. With my panic problem, the thought certainly scared me. But that message put an end to my apprehensions. I told Mei I would be happy to go to China with her.

In the meantime, Mei decided it was time to get her driver's license. It wasn't so simple as needing to transfer a Chinese license. She couldn't drive at all because she had never needed to do so. She rode her bicycle the five miles to work every day.

So I gave her road lessons, and it was funny because if I tried to tell her to stop quickly by yelling, "*Brake! Brake!*" she had no clue what that meant (until after we ran over that unfortunate Boy Scout troop). And I couldn't tell her to "hang a U" or "don't be a lead foot," because she couldn't fathom any kind of American slang. Once I told her to "use elbow grease," and she slapped me. But I was patient. She learned. She studied the driver's handbook, and to everyone's surprise, she got her license on the first try!

Since Mom seldom used her car, a Hyundai (or maybe it was an Edsel), I gave the car to Mei, with Mom's consent. She was still smart enough to know this meant Mei could go to the store for her. Now Mei had wheels and was on her way to becoming an independent Western woman. As for me, Mei had been one of the few women who looked up to me. Would she still feel the same if she no longer needed me as before?

ELEVEN
FREDDIE GOES EAST, Part One
(Or: CHILLIN' IN JILIN)

I'm kind of strange, in case it isn't obvious. Mei wanted us to vacation to China during Chinese New Year, which was celebrated the last week in January 1998 (for some reason it changes every year). But the timing was not good for me. Our trip would have coincided with the Super Bowl, and I wasn't sure I would get to see it in China.

Mei didn't think that was a good enough reason to miss Chinese New Year. But I argued, "They have had 5,000 Chinese New Years. How many more do they need? But there have been only 31 Super Bowls!"

I won the argument. Actually, I think Mei wanted to watch that Super Bowl — her first — and she really enjoyed the game. It was Denver vs. Green Bay, which was one of the few Super Bowls at the time that went down to the wire.

So we booked our flight for the first week in February.

What follows is a travel article I wrote for *The Post and Courier* in 1998, reprinted with permission.

This piece, having been written for a daily newspaper, does *not* include the dreadful time I had trying to "go" on a moving train, as mentioned in this book's preface. That experience will be detailed in all its glory following the article, along with something else that wasn't fit to print in a family newspaper.

From *The Post and Courier*, April 18, 1998:

FAR EAST OFFERS OLD, NEW SURPRISES

By Fred L. Smith

Of The Post and Courier staff

China's top attraction is not the Great Wall — it's the great people.

While in northern China visiting my wife's family, I was overwhelmed by the warmth and kindness of not only her relatives, but nearly everyone I met halfway 'round the world.

Though while traveling in China you'll find it's definitely BYOBP (Bring Your Own Bathroom Paper), almost all of your other needs will be catered to. From massage therapy to fine dining, the Chinese aim to please.

It's not easy getting to China. It involves passports and visas and long flights (18 hours) and lots of patience. But once I got there it was a snap because my wife, Mei, her parents and her three brothers handled everything. I just had to go where they told me to go and stay where they told me to stay. Since I don't speak the language, I couldn't argue with them.

Nor did I need to. They treated me like a king in Beijing. And everywhere else we went.

The Chinese have a great sense of style and color. Nowhere is that more evident than in Beijing, the country's capital, a sprawling metropolis of 30 million people.

Here the old China gives way to the new. Modern hotels, office buildings and architectural wonders rise up from the fruit stands, rickshaws and ancient temples that still remind visitors of the country's rich 5,000-year-old history.

Beijing is one of the world's most beautiful cities, especially at night, when the cityscape, with its myriad multicolored lights, more resembles an amusement park or even Las Vegas than a city in a Communist country.

Despite the abundance of neon, there's no forget-

ting this is China. In nearly every storefront door-
way hangs one of the decorative, orange Chinese
lanterns, which the locals call hong dongs.

With a billion people in a land mass not much
bigger than the United States, it's no surprise China
is crowded. The streets are filled with people, cars
and bicycles. There seems to be just as many people
riding bicycles as driving cars in China. The cyclists
even get their own lanes, but they don't necessarily
get the right of way. No one does. At an intersection,
whichever gets there first, car or bike, wins.

Part of our stay was spent at the Hua Rong Ho-
tel — circular, new and with every modern conve-
nience except that the beds are a bit hard and the
best you can get for breakfast is rice soup and warm
milk. (Blech!)

The hotel seems overstaffed — there's a uni-
formed doorman outside even though the doors
open automatically, and on each floor there sits
a lonely person at an information desk. But that's
pretty much the norm in China. No labor short-
age here. There are always more people on hand
than what you might need, but at least people are
employed and can put the money they earn back
into the economy.

In fact, despite the growing number of jobs in China, the competition for those jobs is so keen that each employee feels pressure to be No. 1, the best at what he does, for there are thousands of people waiting to take his place. Thus, there are no slackers here. Everybody is working at a high level of professionalism.

A surprise for me was the shopping. It turns out it's sensational. The stores are jammed with everything from cameras to leather accessories to bedroom sets to chocolate malts.

Need something? Try a 10-floor department store, loaded with the same merchandise you can find in the West. Just want to look around? Check out the awesome malls (built up, not out). They are even more elaborate and beautiful than the ones here.

Unlike the USA, however, most merchants are willing to dicker on the price, and you may walk away with the best bargains of your life. With an 8-to-1 yuan-to-dollar ratio, I purchased a pair of glasses for the equivalent of 25 American dollars, including the frames, lenses and examination (although the guy who examined me worked out of a briefcase in the back of the store).

Moreover, the store employees are friendlier and more helpful than is typical in the States. And there are so many of them! Every 10 feet stands a salesperson, eager to help you. Try finding even one salesperson when you need one in America.

Despite the modern look of some of the stores, the old China still surfaces. On more than one occasion I saw a store employee using an abacus to take inventory. Some things die hard.

Also, it should be noted that while you might find some good buys in the smaller clothing shops, don't count on a dressing room. When I wanted to try on a pair of pants, it was suggested I sit behind a small desk to change. It's hard to find privacy in a country of one billion people. (On the subject of clothes, the Chinese people for the most part dress the way we do except not as casually. I saw no funny little triangle hats or people walking around in their pajamas.)

The best thing about Beijing: the restaurants. They're superb. They combine Asian atmosphere with excellent staff and out-of-this-world food. Step inside any one of these establishments and it doesn't take long to realize this ain't your daddy's Chinese restaurant. This is the genuine article.

The waiters and waitresses are usually decked

out in bright, colorful uniforms and are on hand virtually every moment of the meal. Take one swallow of tea and they're pouring more into your cup as you put it down. (But don't ask for ice — they probably don't have it.)

No tipping, please. However, if you're willing to pay a little extra, most restaurants offer private dining rooms, whether for a party of five or 50. And karaoke is an indelible part of the scene.

I was told that if you ate a different Chinese food each day it would take 1,000 years to sample every kind. To the Chinese, food is an art form. Once I got the hang of my chopsticks, I was tasting all kinds of new and wonderful things. As well as some bizarre things, such as snake (don't try this at home), some familiar things, such as pork and chicken, and some awful things, such as cold apple soup (sliced, soft apples in water). But always that Chinese staple, rice, was on hand. They just eat it plain.

A word of advice if you go: Do not ask for a hot dog. You might get the real thing!

The Chinese take a communal approach to dining. Everybody eats from the same dish. Every five minutes, a new dish — usually something spectacular — is brought out for members of the dining party to sample.

Now, a little more about bathrooms: I don't ask for much, but a toilet seat would be nice. But often in restaurants and in other places, the restroom consists of a hole in the floor. This can get a little tricky.

Two must-sees in Beijing are the Forbidden City and Tiananmen Square.

The Forbidden City, brought into focus for Americans in the 1987 Oscar-winning film, "The Last Emperor," served as the imperial palace of the Ming and Qing dynasties. It is more than 500 years old.

Set aside a full day to take in the grandeur of this place. It's the largest and most complete imperial architectural compound existing in China. There are several dozen courtyards and more than 9,000 rooms containing large amounts of relics and artistic works. Steer your wife away from the Hall of Jewelry. After getting an eyeful of this stuff, she'll never be satisfied with a mere diamond again.

The shocking, history-making events in Tiananmen Square nearly a decade ago seem a distant memory when strolling the peaceful, spacious square today. Intricately designed kites can be seen *floating above as tourists and locals enjoy the chilly afternoon.*

My sightseeing tour of Beijing also included Tiantan (the Heaven of Temple), where emperors offered sacrifices to heaven and prayed for good harvests. As one of the major historic and cultural sites under state protection, Tiantan has become the symbol of Beijing. It is another link to the country's glorious past.

An 18-hour train ride north of Beijing is Jilin City, my wife's hometown. Along the way I got to see some of the beautiful countryside. Though the farmers and other villagers in the rural areas appear to be living in another century, I heard that even in the small, brick huts you'll find color TVs and stereos — but no cable yet.

Jilin City, which gets mighty cold in the winter (I think it warmed up to 10 degrees one day), is heavily polluted, old and crammed with one million people. With a staggering 20 percent unemployment rate, it's one of China's neglected cities. That will change, for Jilin City is one of the more than 100 cities the Chinese government has targeted for restructuring.

For now, Jilin City is not much of a tourist spot (I was the only Westerner I saw during my week's stay), although the people are as nice as ever and there are still plenty of good shopping and restaurants. And most of the year there is skiing and ice skating.

Even highly successful people with important jobs might live no better here than a family earning less-than-average wages in America. Because of over-population, if a Chinese person is lucky he might be able to rent a small apartment on the fourth floor of what looks like a tenement building, with no elevator and no lights to help him walk down the stairs at night. He'll live behind a steel door. There'll be no sink in the bathroom and no tub. He'll take his showers in the laundry room via a hose with a showerhead attached.

But the people are generally happy here. They know no other way of life. They stick together, work hard and play mah-jongg tirelessly.

The family unit is of prime importance. Respect for others is taught at an early age. Of course, education is stressed. Children sometimes go to school on Sunday, and there is homework even during the summer break.

For the most part, people here are not politically minded. Less than 2 percent of the Chinese population are members of the Communist party.

My favorite memory of Jilin City, aside from the kindness and support I received from Mei's friends and family, is the head-to-toe massage I was given at a sauna by a Chinese woman with magical fingers. It was 55 minutes of heaven for just 12 dollars.

Near the end of my trip it was back to Beijing, where a two-hour car ride on the expressway (with a posted speed limit of 100 mph) brought us to one of the original seven wonders of the world: the Great Wall.

I can imagine some tourist asking for directions to the Great Wall. He would be told, "You can't miss it. It's that 800-mile-long thing to the left."

The Chinese have a saying that translates as: "Not a plucky hero until one reaches the Great Wall." I didn't feel like a plucky hero, but I did feel moved and awestruck.

The entry point we chose (there are some 50 entry points for tourists along the wall) was nestled in the most majestic mountains I have ever seen. Here people from many countries gathered, and I'll bet most of them felt goose bumps as they approached perhaps the greatest engineering triumph in human history.

The Great Wall, with a history of more than 2,000 years, was built as a military defense project. It starts from the Yalu River in the east and meanders through the mountains, valleys and deserts to reach the snow-covered Tianshan Mountains in the west.

According to the Chinese, if you took all the bricks and rocks used in the centuries-long construction of the Great Wall and built a wall one meter wide and five meters high, it would stretch completely around the Earth.

The view is magnificent of course, but after some hard, steep climbing in 20-degree weather, it didn't take but a couple of hours for this plucky hero to say, "I've seen enough."

But one thing about the Wall is that it's still visible even an hour after leaving the entry point.

The Great Wall is not only the pride of China; it's a symbol of the hard working and enduring Chinese people.

It's almost impossible to visit China and not be changed by the experience. The people I met, the *places I saw, the culture I became immersed in all have made a profound impression on me.*

At the very least, I'll never look at a pair of chopsticks the same way again.

FREDDIE GOES EAST, PART TWO

Of course the article didn't get into a lot of personal stuff about Mei's family, and there was no mention of my railroad "rest" stop detailed in the preface. But since this is a book and not a family newspaper, you lucky readers will get all the scatological details in the next few pages.

I was happy to meet Dan Dan, who had just turned ten — or eleven, if you're living in China (don't ask), and I found her to be cute, well-behaved, and bright. We got along very well *before* she came to America, though all was not so idyllic *after*.

Mei's father was well-spoken, serious, and authoritative but nice. He threw three banquets in my honor. Ten years earlier, that would have struck terror in my heart. But I handled everything with surprising ease.

Mei's mother was a beautiful woman, full of life and energy and always smiling. One time we found ourselves alone in a room. Since neither of us could communicate verbally, we just looked at each other, shrugged our shoulders, and sighed.

Mei's brothers were great. I can't pronounce their names. To this day I still refer to them as Brother No. 1 (the cool one, an actor and TV reporter, and great with the ladies); Brother No. 2 (the nice one; well-mannered, with a young son); and Brother No. 3 (the funny one; charismatic personality, lots of girlfriends, too).

I also wasn't able to relate in the article my sheer disgust at a bathhouse Mei's family and I visited. I was given a rubdown, head to toe, by a muscular Chinese guy. That didn't bother me so much. But I got grossed out after he finished and I watched the man rinse off the rag — the rag he had used to scrub my ass — with just a little water. Then he proceeded to use that same rag on the next customer. I wondered how many unclean men he had rubbed down before me, and how many of their germs I was carrying on my person.

At that same bathhouse, I went into a pool with several Chinese men and *was pinched on the butt*. At least, I *thought* that's what happened. I turned around to view the culprit and there was nothing there, except a hole in the wall big enough for a man to put his hand through. So is that what happened, or was it merely the suction from the hole in wall which tickled me when I placed my backside near it? No, dang it, it felt like three fingers and a thumb. To this day I'm not sure and might even be in a state of denial.

Since we're delving into sick and disgusting things, here are the gory details regarding the train trip to Jilin City:

For three days I had held back, but I could wait no longer. It was the middle of the night. Mei directed me to the "restroom," which was just an area behind a door, with a little hole in the floor. This was the restroom? The light from the room shined through the hole and illuminated the railroad tracks passing beneath me. I pulled my pants all the way down, as one is supposed to, I thought. I squatted. Well, I had been drinking; that combined with the train car rocking back and forth plus the imminent explosion from my bowels made this a seemingly impossible task. How could I avoid hitting my pants? I was too drunk and too cold to think of just taking them off. As I felt the cold air rushing up my ass, I took a moment to ponder this truly surreal experience.

After some deft maneuvering, I somehow managed to avoid ruining my pants. When I told Mei about my hard time, she said I was supposed to pull my pants down only to my knees, to avoid just the problem I encountered. Oh well, live and learn.

One last note: I met a journalist over there whom Brother No. 1 was dating. She spoke English very well, and we had a discussion about how the news is covered in China. I made the point that, in the West, if an American politician gets caught with his fingers in the wrong pie, he is exposed in the media. But this is not so in China. It is covered up.

She agreed, but said that the people in the Chinese news media, which is run by the government, are simply used to the way things are and the smart ones don't make waves. The "dumb" ones could find themselves out of a job, or worse. I was told of a Chinese newsman who reported something he was told not to cover. Because of that, his son was not allowed to go to college.

The situation is improving, but Chinese journalists still have that sword over their heads.

TWELVE
HOME ALONE

I was never so glad to come home, and due to a quirk of time change, I was able to leave China at ten a.m. Tuesday and arrive in Atlanta at ten a.m. Tuesday. The first thing I did was go to a Sonic Drive-In and buy myself a foot-long chili dog.

But I picked up a nasty case of bronchitis while in Jilin City, probably caused by the air pollution. I still had some Chinese medicine (little yellow pills) that Mei had given me before I left for America. One thing about Chinese medicine: It either works wonders, or it kills ya!

As planned, Mei remained in China to spend more time with Dan Dan. I was on my own again, so I did "single man" things: I watched cartoons, drank beer (not that I didn't do those things when Mei was around), and burped and farted to my heart's content. But as pleasant as those things were, my burps rang hollow.

Going back to work after three weeks off was tough, and being sick on top of it was miserable. But I regaled my co-workers with stories of my Asian adventure, joking that I briefly joined the nefarious Chinese crime organization the Tong and had to fight my way out. After a few days I was feeling better, and things were back to normal.

I wasn't lonely because my mom was home with me, but she was not the woman she used to be. Her world was slowly shrinking. She seldom left the house, and with her arthritis and decreasing mental capabilities, it wouldn't be long before she could no longer drive. Short-term memory loss caused her to repeat herself.

For almost all of my life, my mom cared for me. She cooked my meals and washed my clothes. Slowly, it was turning around. Within a few years, the roles of parent and child would reverse. I didn't know it at the time, but my mom's senility was already full-blown Alzheimer's Disease.

THIRTEEN
THE IMPOSSIBLE DREAM

Mei returned April 1, 1998, and swore it had nothing to do with April Fool's Day.

We settled into our married routine again. But we knew something was missing. Now it was time to get serious with our campaign to get Dan Dan out of China, so we could be a family.

We had already made the request through U.S. Immigration. The best way to describe Immigration's speed is on a cosmic scale: "and the Earth cooled ... ." It is *that* slow. The problem wasn't with the Chinese government. They were willing to let her go. It was the American government that was hesitant, or at least cautious. All the paperwork had to be in order.

In the meantime, Mei wanted to start working. In fact, she *had* to start working. Trips to China, outings to the movies and dining, plus my obsessive-compulsive desire to add rare comic books to my collection, were taking their toll on our finances. The credit card debt was mounting.

Mei didn't feel comfortable yet working where English was the dominant language, so she got a job at a Chinese restaurant. During her first week on the job, I took several of my ex-girlfriends (well, women I sort of knew, vaguely) to have lunch at the restaurant and check out how Mei was doing.

But working as a waitress and cashier were humbling experiences for Mei. She had been an emergency room nurse in China, and this was a far cry from that. Customers were rude and the tips were small. She also was forced to endure the continuous drama going on among the restaurant staff.

Here's the difference, according to Mei, between American employees and Chinese employees: With Americans, if worker A tells worker B that worker C is stupid, but not to say anything, worker B will go to worker D and say that worker A said worker C was stupid. With the Chinese, worker B will go directly to worker C and say that worker A said she was stupid, *just to cause trouble*. That kind of game seems to make life interesting for them, but Mei wanted no part of it.

Going back into nursing was an option, but because of the differences in technology between East and West, Mei would have to practically start her education all over again. So she remained at the restaurant indefinitely.

All too quickly 1998 rolled into 1999, and still we saw no action from Immigration. Mei's mother became deathly ill, so Mei had to make another trip to China. In Chinese hospitals, the families watch over the patients. Mei and her brothers kept night-long vigils. Thankfully, her mom recovered. I saw a video of the hospital room, and it was like watching an old "Ben Casey" episode: no fancy diagnostic machines, just bare walls.

I called Susan and told her I wanted to send flowers to Mei on Valentine's Day. But she told me there was no way to do that in China. Florists would not take your credit card number over the phone and deliver flowers to your loved one.

After Mei's return, again without Dan Dan, I was forced to sell part of my beloved comic collection to help pay down our credit cards. I sold valuable first editions of *Spider-Man*, *X-Men*, the *Hulk*, the *Fantastic Four*, and numerous others.

This was part of the growing-up experience for me, but it was no easy decision. Let me try to explain why those old comic books meant so much to me. When I was a kid, comic books were one of the joys in my life and a real comfort for me, especially since I had always felt like a misfit. I was small for my age. I had buckteeth. I was emotionally about two-thirds of my chronological age, and I had the huge problem of the panic-attack syndrome always hanging over my head.

So I couldn't wait to lose myself in the monthly adventures of Spider-Man, the Fantastic Four, and all the super heroes from Marvel Comics. Spider-Man, especially, showed me that you could be a misfit and have problems and still triumph at the end of the day.

Unlike most of the other comics on the stands, Marvel Comics were written more for older kids and adults. During Marvel's heyday in the '60s, it was reported that 2,000 college professors subscribed to the comics.

Particularly impressive to me was the art of the unchallenged king of comic book artists, Jack Kirby, who worked on just about every Marvel comic book at the time. His dynamic images virtually leapt off the pages and thrilled me to no end.

When my parents took Cindy, Jeff, and me out shopping and gave us the money to buy ice cream cones, I always passed on the cone in favor of a comic book. The memories of those times are so strong that I can look at the cover of any comic from that era and be transported back in time as feelings of warm nostalgia fill my mind. I not only remember where I bought each comic, but also whether it was night or day and if it was raining or cold.

You don't just toss away those kinds of sweet memories without being affected. Luckily, within a few years I was able to get all those comics in digital form on CD-ROMs. It's still hard to believe that today they're making $100 million movies of those simple superhero morality tales I read as a kid. Comic book heroes have become our new mythology. I was right!

But we had to focus on our present situation. Again we found ourselves at the local Immigration office in downtown Charleston pleading for some word on the status of Dan Dan's case. There was a woman working there at the time, Pi Crankcase (not her real name), who was possibly the rudest, meanest, most intimidating person on the planet. She seemed to delight in keeping poor immigrants who had nowhere else to turn under her thumb. I had fantasies of placing Miss Crankcase's head in an iron vice and slowly squeezing it until her eyeballs popped out. There was no way she was going to help us.

We then took the fight to the offices of Strom Thurmond and Fritz Hollings, our U.S. senators at the time. We got nowhere. I was even told by one of the staffers it would be three years before we could get Dan Dan here. And Mei's boss at the restaurant, who was also a Chinese immigrant, predicted it would be *ten years*!

I refused to accept this. I couldn't stand to see Mei so upset and our lives put on hold. Each day was a struggle to cope. When a dear friend of mine, Betsy Cantler, asked me how the case was going, I was too choked up to answer her.

I made a last-ditch effort to get some official help by writing Congressman Mark Sanford (this was long before the more-recent "Argentina mistress" unpleasantness during his term as governor of South Carolina). But instead of mailing the letter, I gave it to my friend Sybil Fix, a *Post and Courier* reporter. She knew somebody who was close to Sanford, and she gave the letter to him.

Sanford was hand-delivered my letter. Rather than just say "ah, it's hopeless" as the others had done, Sanford's office went to work on it.

I'll never forget the day in May of '99 when I received a call at work from Sanford himself. He told me he had been in contact with the American Immigration office in China.

It seemed they sent two letters to Mei's family indicating that her visa request was accepted, but those letters were lost in the mail, which is typical in China. Now, he said, everything had been straightened out. Dan Dan was getting her visa!

I was overwhelmed by his kind attention and promised Sanford the next time he ran for office he would get my vote. And indeed, when he ran for governor in 2002, I was there at the ballot box. I did my part in helping Sanford win the election. I have to say I don't care what Sanford has done before or since. He's a good man.

I raced home to tell Mei the good news. She wasn't on Cloud Nine; it was more like Cloud 6,592! We still had work to do and forms to fill out, but the wheels were in motion and this time there was no doubt.

Once again, Mei hopped on a plane for China. Only this time, she would be returning with Dan Dan. We had her bedroom all ready, and while I was waiting, I bought her a bicycle and placed it in the center of the room. I daydreamed about outings to the beach and amusement parks.

In a few short days, a plane would arrive carrying mother and daughter. And I would be a daddy for the first time. But sweet irony was waiting in the wings again.

FOURTEEN
PLANNED PARENTHOOD

The plane touched down in Atlanta in early August of '99, during Week One of the NFL pre-season (I can't help it; that's how I remember things).

I saw a very happy Mei and a very tired Dan Dan approach me through the gate. I gave Dan Dan a big hug and a bag of candy. I felt that her teeth should be rotten like the American kids'.

While in Atlanta I took them to Six Flags Over Georgia. But believe it or not, we never left the parking lot. As soon as they saw the huge roller coasters they both begged me to take them away. So much for amusement parks. Dan Dan didn't like the beach, either. I told her she was acting like something of a stick in the mud, and she thanked me.

But she made me feel good when we finally made it home and she took her first glimpse of her new, American-style room, with her own TV, CD player, and VCR. She hugged me and said "thank you." The bicycle I had bought her, though, would only be ridden two or three times. Dan Dan didn't like going outside.

And so Dan Dan began her new life. There were some good times at the beginning but, unfortunately, the fun didn't last long. Dan Dan was due to enter the seventh grade a mere fourteen days after she arrived. This was a very scary time. Dan Dan's English was virtually nonexistent. She would be thrown to the wolves, so to speak.

Before she started Goose Creek Middle School I made the mistake of showing her Three Stooges tapes. She loved them, but when she went to school that first week she did impressions of Curly (you know: "whoop-whoop-whoop," "nyuk, nyuk, nyuk"). Her classmates, who weren't up on the Stooges, thought this was some weird kind of Chinese language! Then they started making fun of her.

It was extremely hard on Dan Dan the first few weeks. Many nights she cried herself to sleep. But the level of schoolwork was not as tough as it was in China and slowly she began to understand and adapt, and the teasing eased off.

There were funny incidents. She came home from school one day and told me, "Daddy, they wrote a dirty word on a piece of paper and tried to make me say it, but I wouldn't."

"That's great, Dan Dan," I replied. Curious, I

asked, "Can you tell me what the first letter of the word was?"

"Yeah, *fuck*," she answered. Talk about a supreme LOL moment.

And what about me? Well, I had a problem dealing with this whole parenthood concept. It was not what I thought it would be. I wasn't enjoying it; it was difficult. I was disappointed in Dan Dan because instead of being the perfect angel I had envisioned, she was just a typical pre-teen: She was lazy, she didn't eat her food, every now and then she was disrespectful to her mother, she lied, she refused to wash the dishes when asked, and she stayed on the computer day and night. In other words, she was *normal*. However, she was also superior in many ways. She was a rare beauty, highly intelligent and a gifted artist. And she had a good heart.

Dan Dan struggled to seek my approval and cope with her brave new world, but because of the language barrier and my inability to relate to a pre-pubescent girl from China, we were not able to bond.

When my sister, Cindy, came to visit from Cincinnati and took stock of all the changes, she said to me, "Well, I guess you're finally happy." But I had to admit, I wasn't. Sure, there were moments of joy and contentment, but overall my feeling was that maybe I just didn't have the capacity to be happy.

Eventually, my sister moved back to Charleston. I found that she had made significant growth as a responsible adult, and she saw the same in me. We became much closer.

During a vacation in Orlando with Dan Dan and Mei, I was having anything but fun. I was bored! Neither Mei nor Dan Dan wanted to go on the big rides. I was just childish enough to let this bother me. Later, I argued with Mei about something stupid, and we both went to bed upset.

I stayed awake half the night, pondering my situation. I really didn't feel the problem was with Dan Dan or Mei. It was with me.

I didn't blame them because I wasn't having a ball. Maybe I wasn't cut out to be a family man. I started to think of the year 1996 as "the good old days," when I was unmarried and could go where I pleased and say what I pleased and do what I pleased. But, in reality, the reason I longed for those days was because I was a still a child then. We all think fondly of our childhood. Mine just happened to last forty-two years!

I knew I couldn't turn the clock back. So I decided to stick it out. I had to give our new family every chance to strengthen and grow. If I didn't, I'd find myself back in my room with my monster movies and Jujubes and feeling mighty foolish.

FIFTEEN
THE TEST

We had decided some months earlier to have a baby, and as a new century dawned, there was a sense of urgency for me. For whatever reasons, I wasn't satisfied being a stepfather. So maybe having a child of my own would fulfill my needs. Mei, too, wanted more.

Well, we certainly tried. But I was forty-five years old, a quarter-century past my prime. Did I have the ammunition?

Meanwhile, life went on. We have a slight problem with hurricanes on the South Carolina coast. In 1989, Hurricane Hugo hit us head on. The city of Charleston and surrounding areas were devastated, and it took years to rebuild. Looking back now though, this was a breeze compared to what those poor folks felt a few states west of us when Katrina blasted New Orleans in '05.

But, anyway, we're a little worried about hurricanes around here. So in September of '99, when Hurricane Floyd gave Charleston "A Close Shave," as the headline said on the front page of *The Post and Courier*, we were understandably nervous beforehand. Nobody knew for sure whether it would be a direct hit, so Mei and Dan Dan joined the mass evacuation while I stayed behind to work at the paper.

What a mess! As everyone was leaving at the same time and state officials refused to open up all east and west lanes of Interstate 26 to outgoing traffic, Mei and Dan Dan got caught up in the longest traffic jam in U.S. history. It took them 13 hours to inch along the 200 miles from Goose Creek to Greenville. They had to leave the unmoving car every now and then to relieve themselves in the nearby woods.

Even more interesting weather arrived in January. It snowed, on back-to-back days from two different storm systems. That was not just highly unusual for Charleston; it was the first time in recorded history. We all loved it, and it reminded Mei and Dan Dan of their chilly days in Northern China.

That same month Dan Dan had a birthday party, and lots of her classmates attended and showered her with gifts. It seemed like Dan Dan was over the hump.

We went to Las Vegas and the Grand Canyon in

April. I tried to explain the Grand Canyon to Mei before we left. But she had no visual image of it in her mind as we Americans do, even those who have never seen it. I said, "It's like this giant *hole*." She really didn't think it was a big deal, but once she saw it, she was blown away.

Mei loved Vegas as well. But being a frugal Chinese woman she only let us lose about $150 at the gambling tables (it took five minutes).

Many people in China believe Las Vegas is a typical American city. When Mei first sent home pictures from Charleston, a quaint, historic city that is anything *but* Vegas-like, her family asked, "Where are all the skyscrapers? Where are the bright lights?"

In May, a local TV station did a feature on Internet romance. Mei and I were the focus of the piece. We got a kick out of being on television, but Mei was upset because I was shown much more than she was. Of course, I don't blame the producers of the segment for this; they naturally picked the most interesting and photogenic person of the two. So she got back at me by telling me I looked bad on TV. "You should have turned around. They showed your bad side," she said. My "bad side?" Up until then, I didn't know I had a bad side.

Summer rolled around, and I decided that something must be done about our financial situation. So I turned over the reins to Mei. I figured she couldn't do any worse than I had. She was now the boss of the money. She paid all the bills, took my credit cards and paycheck away and only gave me money for gas, food, and beer (the three essentials).

Even though it was hard to grow accustomed to this, I gradually began to like it. If you have no money in your pocket, it frees you. For example, I didn't have to worry about whether I could afford taking Mei out to dinner. It was Mei's call. On our anniversary, I'd ask her how much money she wanted me to spend. She'd give me "x" amount of dollars, and I'd spend it on her. It made life simple.

After assuming control and gaining some understanding of monetary matters, Mei was shocked by high-interest credit cards and especially thirty-year home loans. She couldn't understand why we Americans would pay up to three times a home's value and extend the payments to thirty years. In China, homes, or, more realistically, apartments, were purchased with cash. Usually extended family members chipped in to buy a young couple an apartment, and then the couple would reciprocate later. Or companies would give apartments to employees. As for cars, they were also bought with cash. No finance charges, no bills, no banks involved. That's slowly changing, however.

In late July, Mei, Dan Dan, and I were dining at California Dreaming just off the Ashley River. Mei started feeling nauseated. She went to the bathroom and threw up. I took it to be a virus.

Her period was late, so I bought a home pregnancy test. She was alone in the bathroom and *voila*! She saw the pink line. But it was faint. She told me about it, so I rushed to the drugstore to get another test. This time it was for sure. Mei was going to have a baby! (Now I could finally relax and stop taking those steroids.)

Mei suddenly had mixed feelings. This was another big responsibility on her shoulders. Also, it meant she would be tied to me forever! (Not a pleasant thought.) Dan Dan started crying because she thought all of our attention would go to the baby. As for me, I was singing! And if you've ever heard my singing voice, you'd know I was out of my mind with joy.

So there was finally going to be a "mini-me." Was the world ready for this?

SIXTEEN
ASIAN INVASION!

I came home from work the next day and told Mei, "I've never gotten so many hugs from so many women in one day. This baby thing is cool!" My mom was excited too. It had been twenty-six years since her first grandchild (Cathi, my sister's kid) was born.

Naturally, Mei's parents were overjoyed. I didn't know it, but there were big plans being made regarding them. And as we began to explore the baby stores and get ready for this blessed event, we got a visitor: Mei's No. 2 brother had come to America by way of Los Angeles to find work. He then moved to Charleston to be closer to Mei. He got a job as a cook in a nearby Chinese restaurant. Every buck he sent back to China for his wife and young son was worth eight times that.

We called him "Tom." He was very helpful around the house, and he even cut my lawn. I told people I had a genuine Chinese manservant. But he was always hanging around us because he had nowhere else to go in America. The guy wouldn't leave!

Don't get me wrong: He's a nice person. But poor Tom got off on the wrong foot, especially with my mom. The first Sunday he spent with us, she prepared a real Southern meal of tomatoes and rice, pork chops, and lima beans. When you're visiting from another country, you're supposed to at least try to eat the food, and if you can't stand it, just stop. But Tom not only didn't eat the meal, he went to the stove and prepared his own! This pissed Mom off.

The next day, I called home from work to talk to Mom. But Tom answered the phone (a land line, not a cell). He could barely speak three words of English and he's answering my phone? Can you imagine if I had answered my in-laws' phone while staying with them in China? It's the height of presumption!

A few nights later, I was watching the eleven o'clock news, and I guess Tom wanted to go to bed, on the fold-out couch as usual, which happened to be where I was sitting. I went to use the bathroom during a commercial. When I got back, he had already pulled the bed out. Okay, I can take a hint!

Even though Tom eventually found an apartment, — in a commune-like arrangement, sharing the place with several of his Chinese co-workers at the restaurant (commune-like? Chinese people? Who would have guessed?) — he would come over many days after work, which for him was about 10:30 p.m., and spend the night. He'd bring Chinese videos, and as soon as I'd go to use the ol' bathroom, sure enough I would return to find Tom had pulled the bed out and taken over my TV set and VCR.

Tom was also a real jabberjaw, and he and Mei would get together and talk all night long. Since I didn't understand any of what they were saying, it was just irritating noise to me.

People have often asked me, "Fred, why don't you learn Chinese?" (People have also asked me, "Fred, why do you keep a live newt in your pocket?" But that is an issue for another book.) I tell them that, aside from being mentally slow, I just don't care for the Chinese language. I love French, and Spanish is fine, but with Chinese, you have to do too many weird things with your mouth. This attitude doesn't help when I hear Mei and Dan Dan converse in Chinese, point to me and laugh. When I ask them what they're talking about, they always say, "Nothing!"

But back to Tom: A funny incident happened after a cap had fallen off one of his teeth. All of Tom's teeth are capped because he never lost his baby teeth.

That's not normal, even for China. By adulthood they apparently looked terrible so he had all of them capped. This time one of the bottom front caps got dislodged.

Of course he didn't have a dentist in America, and I knew he wouldn't be covered by my insurance, so I thought we could save money by gluing the cap back on ourselves.

I put some Super Glue on the inside of the cap and placed it over his old tooth. I told him to hold it in place with his finger until the glue dried. But I must have gotten a bit of glue on the outside of the cap, because Tom's finger stuck to the cap, and he couldn't get it off. I had visions of my trying to explain to an ER nurse why I brought in a Chinese man with his finger in his mouth. But he finally pulled his finger free. I am proud to say that the cap stayed in place for years, and I thought seriously of taking up dentistry as a second career. But I knew it would take weeks of study, and I couldn't spare the time.

Another funny incident occurred when Mei and Tom asked me to go the video store and rent a Chinese movie for them. They didn't care which one, just as long as it was Chinese. I didn't even know they carried Chinese movies in the video store, but there they were in the "international" section. So I grabbed one that looked all right.

I brought it home, popped it in the VCR, and the whole gang, along with twelve-year-old Dan Dan, sat back to watch. Well, it turns out it was some kind of gay film with the first scene showing two guys going at it. (I didn't even know they had gay people in China. My God, what *else* haven't they told me?)

I couldn't turn off that VCR fast enough! But, just between us, I caught Tom watching the video later that night.

Although I was keenly aware Mei's brother was far from home and took comfort in visiting us, I still blamed him for a rather distressing bout of food poisoning I picked up in early November of 2000. It was *he* I took to a well-known greasy spoon to treat him to an American-style breakfast. The Chinese generally eat nothing "special" for breakfast, just the same stuff they might eat for lunch, and they are certainly missing out. There are probably close to a billion Chinese who seldom, if ever, enjoy the pleasure of eating blueberry muffins, pancakes, grits, Rice Krispies, corn flakes with bananas, link sausage, cinnamon rolls, oatmeal, pop-tarts, cream cheese on a bagel, etc., etc.

Now, where was I? Oh, yes … if not for Tom, I would never have eaten that corned beef hash! It was I who ended up in the ER, not Tom and his tooth, and I had to have three IVs due to dehydration.

The retching was so severe I tore my stomach and vomited blood. It should go without saying that I am not big on vomiting. It's the worst thing that ever happens to me. I would rather be strapped naked to a cactus and forced to listen to Hall & Oates records than vomit. But this night I must have vomited twenty-five times, and *in front of Mei and the nurses*!

During a quiet moment with an IV still in me and behind closed doors, I told Mei I needed to urinate. Since she was a former nurse she said this would be no problem. She got a pan, though it wasn't a bedpan, and positioned my *wee-wee*. But what she didn't count on was the sheer force of a piss whose time had come! The pee started splattering all over, and then Mei lost control of the situation. Pee went all over the bed, the walls, the floor, some delicate medical equipment, and me! I felt like one of those water hoses that gets away from firefighters. It was a Chinese fire drill!

Boy, that seems funny now, but it sure wasn't funny at the time. We finally got out of the hospital at 4:30 a.m. It was the worst night of my life, even worse than the evening I spent listening to a Jehovah's Witness.

Mei's pregnancy was going fine. Everything was on schedule. You know how pregnant women get weird cravings, like for pickles and ice cream? Well, Mei had cravings for food that was strange to *her*. Once at midnight she pleaded with me to go out and buy her a sausage dog. Her Chinese friends must have thought she was nuts.

In the early spring of '01, my co-workers were nice enough to throw a shower for Mei. We were touched, especially Mei, who didn't get this kind of thing when she had Dan Dan in China back in '88. Being so far from her friends and family back home, Mei really appreciated her new friends. And, guys, if you've never been to a baby shower, check one out. It's not the chamber of horrors you might have thought. It's actually kind of fun, and best of all, they bring *food*.

Mei then broke the news to me that her parents were coming to America to be here for the birth of their grandchild. She waited as long as possible to tell me because she knew I would get stressed out about it.

For Mei, the thrill of having her mother and father visit us was mixed with the fact that she would have six people living in our small house, not counting the baby and her brother, and she would have to perform the equivalent of a high-wire balancing act, keeping her parents happy on the one hand and me from going crazy on the other.

They were scheduled to arrive two weeks before the baby was due. The plan was for her father to stay a month, and her mother two months. I think they must count months differently in China.

Or maybe her parents weren't coming to Charleston at all! A funny thing happened on the way to America: The Chinese travel agency mistakenly booked the couple on a flight to Charleston, *West Virginia*, instead of South Carolina. But we didn't know that when we arrived at the Charleston International Airport to pick them up, and they just were not there!

We were *very* upset when we found out what happened. But can you imagine Mei's folks? Not being able to speak English and waiting in an airport three states away for us to greet them? Those poor people had no idea what had happened. I was told Mei's mother started bawling. Whooooo boy!

But Northwest Airlines was used to this kind of thing. In fact, it happened just about every week. So when they noticed two bewildered Chinese people walking aimlessly in the concourse, they found an interpreter and wasted no time in getting my in-laws on a fast flight to the correct city. Five hours later, they arrived safely, smiling, and no worse for the wear.

We drove them to our house and somehow we all squeezed in. The folks had brought us many beautiful gifts from China, including jade animals, scarves, and artwork. Mei was as happy as I'd ever seen her (bulbous, but happy).

We shared a meal of both American and Chinese dishes. I watched, bemused, as my father-in-law attempted to eat peas, one or two and a time, with chopsticks.

Mei's parents slept on the sofa bed in the living

room and my brother-in-law on the floor. Droopy stayed outside and was not pleased. I tried to get Droopy and Tom to exchange places, but Mei got mad at me.

Unable to sleep, I started counting people and nationalities in my house. My mom and I were the only two Americans, versus *five* people of Asian descent. And so, basically, from that point on, my house became Chinatown.

SEVENTEEN
THE FIRST EMPEROR

Quotes from me during Mei's pregnancy:

"I'm not going in the delivery room with you, Mei."

"All right, I'll go in the delivery room. But I'm not going to watch the birth."

"All right, I'll watch the birth. But I'm not going to cut the umbilical cord."

"All right, I'll cut the umbilical cord."

As these quotes illustrate, I originally just wanted to stay in the waiting room, like fathers did decades ago. But I'm glad Mei and all my female friends coerced me into taking an active role in my child's birth. It's a night I will never forget. (But one thing I refused to do was videotape the event. That's just gross!)

They planned to induce Mei — first the seduction, then the induction, as they say — on April 11, 2001. Having a baby in America in the 21st century was vastly different than it was in China in 1988, when Mei had Dan Dan. St. Francis Hospital in Charleston resembles a swanky hotel (not so in China); she had a room of her own (not so in China), 'round-the-clock nurses (not so in China), and an epidural (not so in China). This was the most amazing revelation of all for Mei. When she had Dan Dan, she just had to tough it out. But with the epidural, she coasted through the delivery.

As for me, it was no secret I desperately wanted a boy, though I'm sure I would have loved a girl just as much … eventually. But I had always dreamed of having a son. Despite the problems I had with my father, we had a terrific relationship. Unfortunately, because his own father died when he was only five years old, my father had no notion of how to raise children based on any previous experience. A boy would give me a chance not only to repeat the strong bond I had with my father, but to correct the mistakes he made and raise a kid who would turn out better than I did.

At the time, I didn't know if there was a God or not. But I thought, "God, if you're there, at least give me this one thing."

The earlier ultrasound was inconclusive. So when it came time to assist with the delivery, I kept my eyes peeled. Even though I could clearly see the testicles, how did I know they weren't some kind of tumor or something? So I asked the astonished nurse about the gender, and she confirmed it for me. My dream had come true. (Better still, my boy was not a mutant like so many people believed.) I clipped the cord like an expert. This was another good test for my tear ducts, and they were in perfect working order.

We had discussed boy names but had trouble deciding. Mei said my favorites — Elvis, Shazam and x=y (squared) — were out. A friend suggested Alexander, then we could call him Xan for short. I liked that, but Mei couldn't pronounce Alexander.

One thing was for sure, his name was *not* going to be Fred. I've *never* liked that name. Have you ever noticed in movies that the guy named Fred always loses the girl to a guy named Nick? People name their dogs Fred. And the Chinese pronounce it "Fled." Lord, *Smith* was bad enough!

Then I saw something on TV about Tom Cruise's son, Connor. That name sounded perfect. If it was good enough for Tom Cruise, after whom I had patterned myself (along with Pee Wee Herman), it was good enough for me. Of course, this was years before Cruise made a fool of himself on talk shows. If only I could be a rich, toned, handsome, talented fool like him!

My middle name is Lee, and Mei's last name is Li. So we used Li for his middle name: Connor Li Smith, the first emperor of the Smith clan.

I had worried about my ability to love someone unconditionally. In fact, I had told Mei there was no such thing as unconditional love. Well, I don't know whether it was programmed into my DNA or not, but within five seconds of Connor's birth I felt nothing but unconditional love for this wailing, scrawny little half-breed. At once Connor became the center of my universe.

A couple of days later we took our son home. Friends and relatives came over to marvel at him. We took videos and hundreds of photos. In case you didn't know, the Chinese are big on pix/video. Every event is recorded. My in-laws even shot a video of themselves in Bojangles'. What a thrill.

That first Sunday, Connor peed in my face. And I wasn't anywhere near him. The kid had range!

I was shocked and disillusioned when Mei said to Connor, "Cootchee cootchee coo." What? All this time I thought *cootchee cootchee coo* was a Western invention!

The next couple of weeks went by quickly. The night before Mei's father was due to leave for China, she and I took him out on the town, as far as that's possible in Goose Creek. We bypassed the annual Conjoined Twins Festival and went to a local hang-out and played pool. Her father had never done it. He benefited from my expert guidance, and Mei only beat us a few times. She was already getting her figure back too, and I noticed a guy looking at her from the bar. I went up to him and said, "Would you believe that woman had a baby two weeks ago?"

He asked, "Oh, is that why you were letting her win?"

"I wasn't letting her win," I replied. "I suck."

With the departure of Mei's father, the house became a bit lighter. It was still a busy place, however. Chinese people I didn't even know were in and out at all hours.

In case you don't know, the Chinese are real party animals. Not *wild* animals, mind you, but they love to socialize. It seems that there is a party for every occasion, including all American and Chinese holidays. This is difficult for me because I'm not big on parties to begin with and have a problem connecting with most of the Chinese men I've met. We just don't "get" each other. I'll make a joke, and they'll simply stare at me. And then I'll say something serious, and they'll laugh.

And I never can remember their names. There was one Chinese fellow from Summerville who turned up at all the parties named "Ping." But I called him "Pong" for about a year.

And Mei doesn't help because she forgets their names too! Frequently Mei would reintroduce me to someone I met at an earlier party. Most people in this situation would say, "Fred, do you remember so-and-so?" But Mei says, "Fred, do you remember *him*?" Of course I don't, so I'll have to joke my way out of it by saying something like, "Oh, yeah, you're that Chinese guy, right?"

However, I am not the only poor American husband who gets roped into these parties. Among our circle of friends there are four or five other American husbands, and we all end up hanging out together, the men in one room and the women in the other. Hey, I just realized that's the way *all* parties are!

That May, I got myself "fixed." I was forty-six years old. One kid was enough. However, had I known how incredible Connor was going to be, I might not have had the vasectomy.

Mei didn't fully understand the procedure at first. She actually thought I could never have an orgasm again. I had to ask her: "Honey, do you think I would just abandon my number one hobby?"

Having children automatically forces most people to grow up. And I certainly began aging quite noticeably during those stressed-out first days and nights. I was starting to learn about the important things in life. And, yes, we did buy a minivan.

More importantly, I finally felt like a real, responsible father. It wasn't just about "me" anymore.

EIGHTEEN
THE MOTHER LOAD

At first, three mothers in one house didn't seem so bad. As the days went by my joy for having Connor swelled. Looking at him, I felt I had given something significant to the world. Before Connor, my greatest legacy was my extensive Popeye cartoon library.

But I would get into arguments with Mei regarding child health issues. Mei would call the doctor at the first sign of a sniffle. Conversely, I'm old school. If a bone is not sticking out, the kid doesn't need a doctor (hyperbole, but you get my point). This was the way I was raised. Except for the necessary vaccines, my parents never took me to a doctor. In fact, for many years I thought our family physician's name was Schmoctor, because every time I told my parents I needed to see a doctor they would always say, "Doctor, schmoctor!"

I felt Mei's over concern bordered on the ridiculous. If it was a cool sixty-five degrees outside, she would wrap Connor head to foot in blankets to protect him going from the front door to the car. I could only mutter to myself, "That crazy Chinese chick."

My mother-in-law was a tremendous help, not only with Connor but also around the house. She was a quaint character, though. She cooked her own medicine on the stove in a bubbling cauldron. The stuff was orange, slimy, and smelled like it came out of a pig's butt. I had a cold once, and she tried to give me a cup of it. I told her I would rather be sick.

She smoked roots on the porch. She bathed in the sink, because that is how she was used to bathing. She grabbed an old VCR I was going to throw away, took the innards out, and made a planter out of it!

Her cooking was practically inedible. Everything was soaked in oil and fried beyond recognition. Her green beans were always limp and burned. And if she did manage to cook something Mom and I liked, she made it for us *every day*, bless her heart.

One time I made the mistake of taking her to a local flea market. It was embarrassing. The Chinese love to barter, but my mother-in-law carried it out to the "nth" degree. She'd pick up any old piece of dime-store junk (which looked exotic to *her*) and try to buy it for next to nothing. Even if a dealer went down to two dollars on a four dollar item, she wouldn't rest until she got it for a dollar. Finally, the dealer would relent, just to get rid of her. Curiously, she would buy a lot of items marked Made in China. The reason: Much of the stuff made in China and shipped overseas never ends up on store shelves in China.

My mother-in-law also didn't care how much *time* it took to get a bargain. The Chinese people I have observed place a greater importance on money than time. My wife might stand in line for an hour to save twenty dollars. A worthy cause, but I'd rather give up the twenty dollars to save the hour. This is probably why I turned over my finances to Mei.

I once sat in a bowling alley for twenty minutes watching the Chinese people in our party argue with the manager over what they perceived as a two dollar overcharge. Granted, for them it wasn't the money; it was the principle. I would have given up the two bucks just to go home, but that's me.

The weeks turned into months, and I was never comfortable with my mother-in-law in the house, mainly because of the language problem. She thought I was stupid, and I thought she was stupid. The reality was we just didn't understand each other. (And she was stupid.)

Not understanding didn't stop *my mom* and Mei's mom from having "conversations." No matter how many times I tried to tell her, Mom just didn't get the fact that Mei's mom couldn't fathom a word she was saying. But she talked to her daily about anything and everything. Mei's mom would just smile, nod, and say, "Okay."

My brother-in-law made frequent visits to see his mother, and their indecipherable voices often continued past midnight. I complained, telling Mei that I wanted a "normal" home where the two of us could be alone and take care of the baby ourselves. But Mei was caught in an "un-winable" situation: She loved her mother, needed her help, and didn't want to tell her to leave. She also was aware of my growing discontent and didn't want her mother to come between us.

Mei wanted her mother to have some fun while she was in America and I agreed. So in September of '01 — one week before 9/11 — Mei, her mom, Connor, and I took a cruise to the Bahamas. The cruise line required us to pay full fare for five-month-old Connor (*why?*), and the four of us were crammed into one small cabin.

The cruise was cool, and the food was as great as advertised. But the mother-in-law and the baby were a bit of a drag. This could have been a romance tonic for Mei and me, but it was not to be.

There was some romance going on in the next cabin, however. The walls were thin, and we heard an obviously young couple going at it all night, every night. The girl was particularly loud. I was amused, Mei was embarrassed, and I don't know what her mother thought. Well, at least *one* couple was having fun at night!

For purposes of sick fantasies on my part, I wanted to find out if the woman in question was good looking. I hung out around their cabin long enough to determine that, yes, she was indeed quite sexy, and I looked forward to her little romps every night.

We returned home to find my sister and niece visiting from Cincinnati to see the new baby. Now the house was more crowded than ever, and since I was still on vacation I couldn't even escape to work. I wanted to scream!

One quick escape I found was to ride my bicycle along some nature trails that were entwined within the more upscale Crowfield Plantation neighborhoods in Goose Creek. (We Southerners like the idea of plantations, but let's not go there.) I took many leisurely bike rides in this area, admiring the homes. I vowed one day that Mei would live in one of those houses. Hopefully, with me. I rode down one trail that came to an abrupt end at the beginning of a neighborhood street. I had to turn around, but as I did, I saw a home next to the trail. It was just another house, I thought. I had no idea I would soon be living in it.

My small concerns were put into perspective as the tragedy unfolded on September 11. Back at work it was controlled chaos, as everyone went into extra-high gear trying to cover this, the greatest news story of our lives, from every angle, locally as well as nationally. We were all huddled around the newsroom TV, trying to digest and process what we were seeing.

Despite the new security surrounding the nation's airports, Mei's mother, her suitcases packed with the flea market "treasures" she had bought here, was able to leave for China as scheduled on the 18th. She had been with us six months. Mei cried, but I was relieved (though I celebrated silently).

I was actually happy for at least a day and a half.

Then I changed my first diaper. From that point on, I knew I was going to have my hands full.

NINETEEN
MOVIN' ON UP

A brief dissertation on diapering:

There are two basic rules.

Rule No. 1: Don't notice the baby needs changing. Let your wife discover it, so she can do the changing. Act surprised.

Rule No. 2: If you have to do the changing, breathe through your mouth. Gag risk is high if you catch a whiff through your nose.

Otherwise, changing diapers was not so bad, depending on the shape and consistency of the "gifts" the baby leaves you. A "pancake" is no problem. Easy to clean. Likewise "meatballs," "biscuits," and "grapes." What you don't want is "oatmeal" or "gravy." These are very messy, stinky, and hard to clean, and they will cause you to utter the Lord's name in vain numerous times.

And now, back to our story … .

Some people can't drive a nail. I can't even hail a cab for a nail.

So when it came to the maintenance of our little

thirty-five-year-old abode, nobody nominated me. But not being handy around the house has its advantages. As my hands have not experienced hard physical labor, they remain wonderfully soft in the bedroom. Just ask Mei. Actually, on second thought, don't.

Through the years, the house had fallen into disrepair. Oh, sure, we painted and fixed some little things, but big problems had developed. Cracks were appearing in the bedroom and living room walls. While outside, the bricks behind the back bedroom were beginning to separate.

We had to get outta there.

To that end, through some miracle of Chinese financing, Mei was actually getting us out of debt. In just eighteen months, she had whittled $10,000 in credit card payments down to $0. When I asked Mei how she accomplished this, she told me it was an ancient Chinese secret. (Say, maybe she laundered the money! Sorry, that was a bad joke.)

At any rate, we could afford to move. And it was Mei's dream to live in an American home of which she could be proud.

But first we had to ditch … er, make that *sell* … our house. We hired someone to fix the back wall, and we tried to make the place presentable. I had a dream that I instructed workers to board up my mom's room, while she was still in there. Mom could be heard banging on the wall, asking for peanuts and teeth. I wonder what the dream meant?

We put the house on the market in December of '01. Nothing was happening by the spring of '02 when some friends of ours were taking a trip to China, and we let Dan Dan go with them. She got a chance to see her father and visit her school and old friends. She quickly realized that her new home in America was where her heart was.

In April, Connor had his first birthday party, which was a real international affair, attended by people from at least four different countries. Here I met Mei's new friend Sheena, a lovely, statuesque Asian woman who would figure prominently in our lives a year later.

In June we thankfully found a buyer and then began house hunting for real. The search didn't take long. There we were in Crowfield Plantation, taking a tour of the most beautiful home I had ever seen. And right next to the house was that very same bicycle trail I had taken a year earlier.

You're not supposed to buy a house out of emotion. We thought we could do that, but Mei and I took one look at this place, and we knew we had to have it. We made an offer the next day and moved in July 2nd. I hired movers because I had been diagnosed early in my life as "heavy-lifting intolerant."

Stately Smith Manor, as I called it, provided us with almost double the space. It must have seemed downright cavernous to little Connor. We now had a large, screened-in back porch, a beautiful yard, which I would surely turn into a jungle in six months, and a two-car garage that we could fill up with junk and never be able to squeeze even one car in. We also had, for the first time in my life, *two bathrooms*. At last, I had an extra place where I could read in peace! What's more, a spare room doubled as my den, allowing me to shut out the increasing Chinese yak festivals.

Dan Dan liked the house a lot but almost never ventured outside. When we would go places in the car, she would exit the house through the kitchen door, which led to the garage. Nobody in the neighborhood ever saw her. In fact, and I swear this is true, the neighbors across the street didn't know we had a daughter for *two years*.

On a sad note, we had to give Droopy away because Mei didn't want the dog to mess up our new house. I reluctantly agreed. Droopy had always been a problem child, and Mei was tired of dealing with her. I put an ad in the paper and two really nice ladies came to pick her up. Droopy seemed to like them.

I was "dogless" for the first time in my life. It was hard to adjust, and Mei kept yelling at me not to give Alpo to Connor. But we did plan to get a small house dog later, when Connor was old enough.

Dan Dan had to change schools again, from Goose Creek High School to Stratford. It's the same school involved in the infamous police drug raid that made all the national headlines in '03. "Saturday Night Live" even did a lead sketch about it a mere two days after it was reported.

The situation went down like this: The Goose Creek police marched into the school hallways early one morning, guns drawn, looking for drugs. But there were none. It was all caught on camera as innocent children were forced onto the floors, guns pointed their way and police dogs howling. Dan Dan was outside at the time and saw nothing. In fact, she didn't find out what was going on until two days later when the incident was all over television.

In any event, Dan Dan handled the adjustment to her new school very well and was only rousted by the cops once or twice. (Oh, I'm just kidding. The nice, friendly Goose Creek Police Department watches over my house at night and will continue to do so, I hope.)

Mom took a while to get used to her new environs, but she seemed all right with the move. Only now she needed help operating the shower faucets. I tried once to assist her with that, but despite numerous precautions on my part, I accidentally saw her naked. So I had to get Mei and Dan Dan to handle it from then on ... or until I was forced to wash her daily, which was coming soon. I remember telling a co-worker at the time, "I will do everything for my mom that I can, but I'm not going to wipe her butt." He replied in a knowing tone of voice, "Yes, you will."

So we were in our dream home. Within a couple of months, Mei took her U.S. citizenship test and aced it. She didn't even have to cheat, as I recommended. When the time came to take her oath, Mei, Connor, and I gathered at the Immigration office in Charleston with people from many different countries. Here Connor held court, running and dancing and playing. He was so funny and charming that it didn't matter where the people came from, they just laughed and enjoyed him.

I was proud to see Mei take her citizenship oath. She had sure come a long way from the scared, homesick, wayward woman-child I found in Greenville. Her daughter was with her. She had a devoted husband and a beautiful son and was now a U.S. citizen.

Everything was perfect, right? It was. For a while.

TWENTY
BAPTISM BY IRE

Though I was brought up Baptist, barely, and even attended the Baptist College in Charleston (now called Charleston Southern University), I was never a deeply religious person. Briefly I was "saved" in the '70s, but it didn't take. I had so many questions the church couldn't answer.

Science, at least, attempted to tackle the tough questions about the origin of the universe and what makes it tick. And science was a self-correcting mechanism, whereas the tenets of the Bible were set in stone.

During my time of greatest personal turmoil in the '80s, I became an atheist, convincing myself of a cold, Godless universe in which life just accidentally emerged. I softened somewhat in the '90s and became agnostic, feeling that if there was a God, he just got the universe started and then must have blown the scene because he certainly wasn't helping out here.

My views would radically change later, but even so I would never care for the dogma of the church, and I couldn't buy the premise that all the beauty and complexity of the universe was summed up into whether or not one accepted Jesus Christ as savior.

Regardless of my feelings, Mei somehow managed to become a Christian just before Connor was born. She went to a church on nearby James Island that had a partly Chinese congregation. She didn't attend regularly, and she really didn't understand the Bible deeply (who the hell does?), but she did believe in God and was attracted to the social scene at church.

I didn't make an issue of it until in the fall of '02 when I saw a home video of Mei being baptized at the church. I was shocked! *My wife was baptized without my knowledge or consent*!

Mei said she hesitated in telling me because she knew I would give her trouble about it. Damn right! But had Mei really understood the implications of what she did, I might have been furious. She didn't, though, and the deed was done so there was no need to be a jerk about it.

But a religious divide was one of the many cracks that were developing in a relationship that already had a cultural and a language divide.

TWENTY ONE
SHANGHAI SURPRISE

More than anything in the world, I enjoyed coming home from work and seeing a smiling Connor run up to me and say, "Da Da! Da Da!" I hadn't felt this way since I completed my collection of *Mad* magazines!

But you know what I enjoyed even *more* than that? Seeing Connor go to bed! He really gave me a workout every night, as Mei didn't get home from the restaurant (or *restaurants*, I should say, as she ended up working for several) until after 9 p.m. Often I felt like taking care of Connor was my second job. It was worth it, but could I survive it?

Then came the long weekends. Most guys think of excuses to get *out* of going to work. I made excuses to Mei to *go* to work, just to get out of having to babysit Connor all day while she shopped or puttered around the house.

"Sorry, Mei," I found myself saying, "but they want me to go to work on Saturday because, uh, there might be a big news story breaking … like a dock worker's strike … yeah, that's it, a dock workers strike!" Believe me, moving a computer mouse around at work is far less strenuous than having a toddler crawl all over you all day, demanding your full-time attention.

I'm kidding ... well, a little bit. I treasured my time with Connor, my one and only son, even though he tuckered me out.

Sometimes I found myself catching naps on the bathroom floor. It was the only way to get a break. If I tried to doze in the bed, Connor would bother me. So I would say, "Da Da go pooh pooh," then I would lock the bathroom door, pull up the soft floor mat, grab a towel for a pillow and at least catch thirty winks, if not forty.

But I made the same mistake with Connor I made with Dan Dan: showing Three Stooges videos. After he watched a pie fight, he quite unexpectedly hit me in the face with a hardback book. And after watching Popeye cartoons, he would pretend to eat his spinach and then pummel me.

You'd think a trip to Shanghai would be the vacation I needed, but it was anything but that.

Mei wanted to bring Connor, now almost two

years old, to the Far East to meet the folks, and she planned to bring her mother back with us for a month-long stay. That was the plan, anyway. It was early March, and Dan Dan stayed home so she wouldn't miss school and to look after my mom.

Once again, we were jetting our way to the other side of the world. It took me forty-eight years to take my third trip out of the country. At the tender age of twenty-two months, Connor already was making his second trip (remember, he had cruised to the Bahamas with us). He was a seasoned world traveler, even if he didn't know it.

Even more than before, the long flight took its toll. Connor was awake and roaming around through most of the flight. We had to constantly stop him from waking people up or grabbing their food. Still, he was precious, as always, and many of our fellow flyers delighted in him.

We hit Beijing first, at about 3:00 p.m. But from our point of view it was 3:00 *a.m.* And of course the relatives were all gathered at the airport, ready to party. They had big plans for us, even though we could barely stand up!

The first day (night?) was a blur of going to see this relative or friend and going to this restaurant or that. Unlike my first Beijing stay, Mei's father was out of town, so I didn't get all those huge banquets that I remembered so fondly from my first trip. No, my palate had to deal with a more limited bill of fare. I knew enough Chinese to say, "wah yow row" (my spelling), which loosely translates to "I want meat."

But man does not live by meat alone, and although I tried some vegetables, some of the stuff was impossible for me to digest. There was a lot of fishy food, too. I could swear someone tried to get me to eat a bowl of plankton!

Most of my time was spent chasing after Connor, trying to prevent any international incidents, while Mei socialized. I was happy to do that for her — after all, I had virtually nothing to say to anyone — but it was hardly my idea of fun.

I tried to send a telegram to Mom to tell her how we were doing in Beijing, but I couldn't find an Eastern Union office.

The first sign that real trouble was in the wind came when Susan, who had since moved to Beijing, asked me why I didn't have a heavier coat for Shanghai. I told her Mei said I didn't need it, since Shanghai was farther south than Beijing, where the temperature was brisk but tolerable. She informed me it was six degrees in Shanghai, without the wind chill. Good Lord!

On the way to the train station, Connor threw up all over me in the cab. He was sick, and I wasn't feeling too great either, having to hold him with vomit all over us for the next twenty minutes. Incidentally, the cab driver apparently was a friend of the family. The next time I saw him was five years later. He came up to me at a party and actually asked if I recognized him. (Fill in your own joke here.)

We got cleaned up and made our way to the train through a mass of humanity. Connor threw up again in our berth. The poor little guy was really out of it. Rather than have to deal with Connor for fourteen hours, along with having to listen to a lot of Chinese banter, I decided to take a half bottle of sleeping pills to zonk myself out until morning.

As soon as I woke up, Connor threw up on me again. This time I had no convenient change of attire so all I could do was scrape the vomit off and hope the smell would go away.

Pulling into Shanghai, I noticed there were a lot of Chinese people there. (Sorry, I just had to slip that joke in.)

Sheena, our friend in Goose Creek, greeted us. She had just moved to Shanghai. Sheena was not only gorgeous (so I had a nice view), but she also proved to be an exceptional tour guide. We didn't know at the time just how much we would need her help.

Shanghai is truly one of the world's most spectacular cities. It seems never-ending. It far surpasses New York City in sheer volume of skyscrapers. The architecture is jaw dropping: very 21st century.

First, we did some shopping at a multi-level mall, and Connor, who was feeling somewhat better, ran around one of the stores. The employees and patrons seemed enthralled by his antics. I think I overheard one of them say, "Holy Buddha! Look at that little boy with the brown hair!" Any hair color other than black attracts attention over there. I always felt I had eyes on me. Everybody thought I was from Russia. I didn't care. China is one of the few countries wherein I am at least close to average height. It's a small consolation, I grant you, but I'll take it.

While the girls were gathering goodies, brother-in-law No. 1 and I went to a doughnut shop (yep, a doughnut shop) and got our first chance to sit down and talk, or whatever we were doing considering his English was limited and my Chinese was practically zilch. But even so, we discussed John Lennon, photography, and our favorite topic, women. Everyone in the shop was staring at us. *Hmmm*, I thought. *Must be something wrong with my brother-in-law!*

The gang got back together, minus Sheena, who had some work to do, and we went up in the Jin Mao Tower, a monolithic, emerald-hued super structure that was awesome in its design and beauty. The center of the building is carved out so visitors can peer down the shaft eighty-eight stories to the ground. It takes one's breath away.

But there was a problem with Shanghai: It was too damn cold. The wind chill put the temperature way below zero, and I just wasn't used to it, being from sunny South Carolina. I'm not a sissy or anything … well, yes, I am. I am a sissy. But as sissies go, I'm the toughest around, and I'll beat the crap out of any other sissy who says I'm not.

Brother-in-law No. 1 insisted we walk around town — near the frigid Long River, no less — to sightsee. At first, I refused to go. But Mei bought me a scarf and hat, and the people in our group shamed me into venturing outside. Of course as soon as we took our first steps, a freezing rain started to fall, which really didn't bother me, as I'm one of the few people who likes sleet.

I'm happy I went because we took some fantastic pictures and videos. I started to get accustomed to the snot freezing around my nose, and I enjoyed walking through some of the quaint streets and shops.

I hit the jackpot when they took me to a DVD store. Every DVD in the place cost anywhere from $1.00 to $1.50. This was back when the average price of a DVD was $15.00, before they started practically giving them away. These were major U.S. films, from modern films such as "Analyze This" to classics such as "The Graduate," widescreen and everything, imported to China with Chinese subtitles that could be switched off. I ended up getting $500.00 worth of DVDs for only $45.00. The only extra cost was the $800 plane fare to China!

Connor was still feeling sick, though we thought he was on the road to recovery. But when we sat down to eat at an authentic *American* restaurant, just as I was ready to dig into my T-bone, Vomit Boy began throwing up again. And again.

We knew this time it was really serious, so we rushed him to the emergency room of a Shanghai hospital. This was an eye-opening experience for me. The walls were cracked and the floors dirty. There were no computers. The staff used index cards and didn't quibble with insurance forms.

With Sheena's help — God bless her — we got Connor some help within fifteen minutes. Maybe we got the quick service because I was American. I'm just guessing.

They determined Connor picked up a virus that was going around (this was just weeks before SARS — severe acute respiratory syndrome — hit big there), and he needed fluids. The nurse put an IV in his head — yes, that's right, his *head*. They do that to toddlers over there instead of using sedatives. Connor wasn't supposed to be able to pull it out, but he did, and my son's blood was shooting everywhere. So they had to put another IV in, and we were told to hold his arms down.

Finally, Connor went to sleep. Mei and I calmed down a little. We waited for the IV to finish until about 2:00 a.m. Sheena was there with us the whole time. I will forever think fondly of her for that.

The next morning at the hotel, Mei had come down with the same virus. Somehow I was spared. So I had two sick loved ones who were unable to leave the room, and I was cooped up in there with them for an entire day. And the TV was all-Chinese except for one news channel that repeated stories over and over. And to top it off, I didn't bring a book to read because Mei said, "You'll be having too much fun and be much too busy to read." Thanks a lot, Mei!

Needless to say, it was a lo-o-o-o-ng day. But by late afternoon, brother-in-law No. 1 and my mother-in-law took me to the "old" Shanghai, which looks about as old as Manhattan. In fact, roaming those streets made me feel like I was in New York City. We went to the Peace Hotel, where many American presidents have stayed. We went on the roof and gazed, wide-eyed across the Long River at the miraculous "new" Shanghai. As scenic as it was, we decided to come back after nightfall to see the city lit up.

I met a fellow American from Seattle who thought it was Saturday. I informed her I knew for certain it was Friday. I found out later that she was right.

Somehow, somewhere, I lost a day. Must've been those sleeping pills.

Mei was feeling better by nighttime. Her mom looked after Connor so we could go out on the town. Sheena joined us. But I was thinking more about that day I lost. It was a good thing. It meant I could go home that much sooner. Though we went to some interesting places, I was just counting the hours. What with the cold, the strange food, and the sickness, it had not been a fun trip. When we went back to the Peace Hotel to see the city lights, we found out *Shanghai was turned off*! It seems they only stay on until 11:00 p.m. or so, and it was just passed that. I felt like I was living in my own, private Year of the Rat.

I spent much of my last day in Shanghai carrying a partially recovered Connor, who was too afraid to walk in the crush of people down the busy city streets while Mei shopped. I hated every moment of it. By the end of the day, I was exhausted.

Another arduous train ride brought us back to Beijing. On the final evening we visited Mei's uncle at his home, and I can truly say I enjoyed my time there. Besides being a gracious host, her uncle, a journalist of some stature, had a home that would knock anyone's socks off. And that was just one of his places. The people who do well in China *really* do well!

Amidst the SARS rumors and talk that some of the flights out of China had been delayed, I was relieved when my plane was finally out of Chinese air space. The last thing I wanted was to be stuck in China indefinitely. But I was now worried about Mei and Connor. They were staying behind for another two weeks. In that length of time, SARS rumors can turn to widespread SARS panic.

TWENTY TWO
HELL WEEKS

Once I got home I realized that SARS (Stupid Ass Redneck Syndrome) was already prevalent in South Carolina. So everything was normal.

I thought to myself, *Boy, it's gonna be great for two weeks not to have a baby crawling all over me, demanding my time and going "waah-waah" at the drop of a hat. I'll have fun!*

Well, I couldn't have been more wrong. Within a couple of days the euphoria of freedom wore off, and I was miserable. I had no idea I would miss Connor so much. It was a terrible feeling, the likes of which I had never experienced, and I found myself sinking into depression.

This pointed to philosophical differences between Mei, her brother, and me. Mei and Tom had left their young children in China to seek brighter futures in America. While I applaud them for their courage and tenacity, I could never leave Connor for any reason, except for a two-week period such as this, and even then my heart had a hole in it.

However, I knew Connor would return to me soon.

I kept myself busy by copying my VHS tapes — one thousand hours worth — onto discs with a new DVD recorder I purchased for $600, since they were new to the market. Now you can buy one for pocket change. This is what geeks do. Only I got obsessed with it. Night and day, if I wasn't copying tapes I was thinking about copying tapes. I wish I could direct my passions to something useful, like world hunger, saving the whales, or eliminating all known references to Don King. At any rate, this kept me occupied and stopped me from crying myself to sleep because Connor wasn't with me.

Mei would call from China and put Connor on the phone. There were three languages in our house: English, Chinese, and Connorspeak.

Me: "Hey, Connor, old buddy. How's it going? This is Da Da. I really miss you. Are you being a good boy?"

Connor: "Gurble preknak hossle frezmat."

Still, this was a much-needed lifeline to my son.

Though Dan Dan had done a good job helping my mom while we were gone, and some friends brought them food from time to time, it was now my job to take over. By this time Mom could no longer cook, just make coffee in the morning, and needed someone to prepare her lunch and dinner. As a cook, I am the antithesis of Emeril, but I can fix simple stuff like eggs and hamburgers. I haven't poisoned anyone enough for him or her to take me to court (yet).

A typical culinary crack-up commenced when I bought a bread maker and tried to make the stuff. The recipe called for something like four cups of flour. But instead, I put in four cups of sugar. The result was a protoplasmic mass, but at least it was sweet.

Dan Dan would do anything to get out of eating my cooking. "I'm a vegetarian now," she announced when faced with one of my "meatloafs."

The next day I saw her eating a hot dog. Some vegetarian! Another excuse was, "I just drank a whole lot of water, Daddy, and I'm full!"

I turned the tables on her the next day. When she asked about supper, I told her we weren't going to have any. "Just drink water like you did yesterday," I said, smirking.

Did I say we had three languages in our home? Make that four. Dan Dan was now conversing in a rapid-fire form of teenspeak, but with a Chinese accent overlay. This was all but impossible to decipher. I realized that teens today talk as if they're asking questions. This is what I hear: "So, like, we saw this movie? And it was, like, really scary? And we, like, covered our eyes, but, like, we could still hear it? So, like, it was still scary? Daddy, are you, like, listening to me?"

We somehow survived each other. At long last, the two weeks ended, and my wife and son returned to me. I had felt like nothing without them.

And yet, later that year I put myself in danger of losing them and everything Mei and I had built together.

TWENTY THREE
THE CHINA SYNDROME

I was happy to have Mei's mom visit us again. No, really! I wanted her to see our new house and enjoy her month with us. But before Mei bought her mother's plane ticket, I insisted that she make it a round trip, not open-ended like last time. That way, I would be able to see on her ticket a definite date of departure. I didn't want a repeat of the last six-month visit.

Mei assured me she would do that, but Mei sometimes made assurances when in fact her mind had been made up to do it another way. It seems to me that Chinese women do a lot of "yes, yes, yes" when they really mean "no, no, no." It's probably their way of avoiding an argument.

Mei confessed the plane ticket was open-ended. Her mother would stay for another six months, or *more*. I knew there had to be a law against this. I looked it up, and yes, there is a little known S.C. statute, which states that a mother-in-law cannot stay at a son-in-law's house for more than a month *if* she's an axe murderer. I thought about getting her interested in chopping down trees, but I figured it would probably backfire on me.

Still, Mei's mother was a pleasant old gal, and we did have fun sometimes. But just as her son, Tom, had caused grievous injury to my stomach and my soul (remember the food-poisoning incident?), my mother-in-law was the culprit in another unfortunate turn of events. She caused me to tear my ACL. That's the anterior cruciate ligament of the knee, for those who don't watch sports.

We were playing badminton, and as I stepped back to hit the birdie, I must have planted my foot wrong. It felt like someone took a hammer and whacked me on the side of my knee. I dropped like a sack of wet potatoes (I don't know what that means), crying out in agony, as Mei's mom *laughed*! She thought I was just kidding around. (Mei reacts the same way when I get hurt. Once, playing softball, I pulled a leg muscle running to first base and collapsed. Somehow, I managed to make it to the bag safely by crawling. I looked up at Mei in the stands. She was smiling. I shouted, "Mei? What gives? I'm hurt!" She replied, "Really? I thought you were just making a *joke*!" Why do people always laugh at me when I am nearly killed?)

Anyway, it was *all* my mother-in-law's fault that I hurt my knee. It had absolutely *nothing* to do with the fact that I was forty-eight years old and never exercised. I couldn't even tell people at work I hurt my knee getting tackled in football or something cool like that. No, I blew out my knee playing *badminton*!

As far as Mei was concerned, her mother could stay forever. Mei loved her and needed her help around the house. Mei felt she was doing it all, and I wasn't pulling my weight with the dishes, the cooking, the clothes, and cleaning. Apparently, my charming personality was no longer enough!

True, I am lazy. One time I grew a mustache, not for aesthetic reasons, but because shaving my upper lip was too much trouble. (Actually, Mei is lazy too. She just covers it up by working hard.)

From her mother's point of view, why *shouldn't* she stay on? She had her daughter, granddaughter, grandson, and a son in America. Maybe, in her mind, that beat a husband, two other sons, and a grandson (Tom's boy) in China.

Did she really want to stay permanently? I didn't know. What I did know was that I felt manipulated by Mei and began to resent her and her mother and just about anything Chinese.

When a person is resentful, he's not too pleasant to be around. I probably made Mei's life miserable during this time. I was always complaining, "showing my bad face," as she called it, slamming doors in anger and spending most of my time in my den away from everyone. I was also getting increasingly irritated at my own mother, even though I knew she couldn't help her mental state.

But back to the marriage: I felt I was no longer in control of my environment. "Too much Chinese," I would think to myself. I felt like a guest in my own home. And I felt like Mei was putting her family's needs over my own. They were always busy doing things, going places, having parties, and generally being a big nuisance to me. I remember at one party I was sitting on the couch alone, watching TV while all the Chinese guests were whooping it up at the dinner table. I said to myself, "Boy, if this were *Survivor*, I bet I'd be the first person voted off this island." The sad truth was that I *wanted* to be voted off. I felt left out and liked it that way. But this attitude put some distance between Mei and me, and made for a good marriage not.

And, hey, Mei wasn't Little Miss Perfect in all of

this. She had grown dissatisfied and had become too bossy and temperamental. I began to call her "my Manchurian malcontent." (Behind her back, of course.) She also developed a new hobby: criticizing me. She even said my appearance was going to pots. Not pot. Pots. I wore pots.

Worst of all, she started looking at other men. I had always looked at other women, but it wasn't my fault. It was that damn DNA of mine.

This was a dark period for us.

We weren't on the doorstep of divorce or anything as drastic as that … *yet* … and we surely shared our love for Connor, but, clearly, we didn't love each other the way we did before.

As our relationship began to unravel, Mei's mother believed she was partly the cause. She moved in with a couple in Mount Pleasant, a town about twenty-five miles away. They needed help with their children. She only stayed with us on weekends. But it couldn't fix the damage that had already been done.

I was beginning to feel like I didn't want to be married anymore. I missed *my* freedom and *my* privacy and *my* money. I was having a "seven-year itch" one year early.

Things came to a head around Thanksgiving of

'03. Mei's brother had car trouble and he tried to talk to the mechanic himself, but who understands a mechanic? Much less Tom, whose English was still pretty limited.

I asked Mei, "Why didn't your brother have me talk to the mechanic for him?"

Mei responded, sternly, "Because he doesn't want to ask for your help. He thinks you don't like him."

I replied: "I like him, I just don't want him *living* here (he didn't, it just seemed like he did). But do you think I would just say 'screw you' if he asked me? If a friend needs help, I help him."

"You don't *have* any friends," Mei shot back before she walked off.

This happened in front of my sister, who was back living in Charleston, along with my niece. I found out later my sister went to Mei, and instead of defending me, said, "Mei, you're right. Fred's an asshole."

So I had become the bad guy. Not just to Mei's family but to mine. But at the time, I didn't think I needed to change. I thought I just wanted to get out.

I came to a crossroads in my life. I had to make a decision. I *knew* I would ultimately choose Mei because it wasn't hard to imagine an empty world without her. But if I chose marriage only half-heartedly, without embracing it with all its trials and tribulations as I should have, it would not have been the kind of marriage Mei wanted. I, in turn, could not stay married to someone who didn't love and respect me.

I didn't realize it, but this "bad" time was a picnic compared to what was going to happen. Yes, things were going to get worse … far worse than I could have imagined.

TWENTY FOUR
THE PROBLEM WITH MOM

It wasn't her fault, but I resented my mom for years because I couldn't get away from her. Except for two brief stints in which I lived on my own, it was as if we were chained to each other. Something always brought us back together. The first time, in 1984, I was living alone in an apartment when my father committed suicide. He was playing Russian Roulette with a .22 pistol and shot himself in the head right in front of a friend. We knew it was suicide and not just dangerous game playing because for years he had talked about killing himself, and his life and health had deteriorated to such a low point that I was not at all surprised when I heard the news. Plus he was an alcoholic who owned a liquor store ... a bomb waiting to explode.

He left my mom nothing, and she only had a part-time job then. So I felt obligated to move back in with her. I didn't mind, however. She was a very pleasant roommate, and besides, she did all the laundry and cooking!

The second time came a few years later. She sold

our house and moved in with her mom. I moved into an apartment on James Island. But it turned out that, in such close quarters, my mom couldn't get along with my grandmother, who,was in the beginning stages of Alzheimer's *herself* at that time. So my mom moved into my apartment. Again, I didn't mind. Did I mention she did all the laundry and cooking?

Feeling cramped, I bought a house of my own in 1991, and of course my mom went with me. Through the next six years, prior to meeting Mei in 1997, Mom's mental state was on a slow decline. Her disease had shifted from the beginning to moderate stages, though I still wasn't even aware she had Alzheimer's at the time, and there was virtually no meaningful communication between us. My patience with her began to wear extremely thin.

If I had a crystal ball and could see what was to come, I would have cherished every cognizant moment with my mom. Her brain was literally shrinking.

By early '04, Mei's mother had returned to China and things were relatively normal again, except that Mom was getting more and more dependent, and she had lost the ability to think for herself. I took her to doctors and heard for the first time that dreaded word regarding my mom: Alzheimer's.

My niece, Cathi, came to the rescue by offering to take Mom in for a while. Cathi, in turn, would receive my mom's Social Security checks, allowing her to afford a fairly nice apartment for them in Mount Pleasant. This would give me a needed break as well as give Cathi some company at night, so the benefits were clear for both of us.

At this point my mom was just very, very forgetful and often confused. But she could still feed and bathe herself, go to the bathroom, and could be left alone while my niece worked.

However, during the nine months she spent with Cathi, something happened. One doctor told me that perhaps she had fallen and hit her head. Regardless of what caused it, she took a dramatic turn for the worse and virtually lost her sanity. She no longer had any control of her bowels, she would eat everything in sight, including Christmas ornaments, paper, and dead insects, and she was incoherent and delusional. She knew who we were, but it was as if she were in a dream. Her reality was very different from ours.

We began looking at a nursing homes for her, but we knew it would take time to find one. I offered to take her back with us at this stage, but Cathi, unfortunately not knowing the scope of matters with which she would have to deal, told me she could handle Mom until we were able to get her into a facility. We were given some bad advice and were under the impression we could get Mom into a nursing home in a couple of weeks. Unfortunately, that wasn't the case.

Unbeknownst to Cathi, one night Mom got out of bed and turned on the water faucet in the bathroom. She left it running all night. The water flowed down from Cathi's second floor apartment into the apartment below.

The next morning I got a frantic call from Cathi. "Fred, my landlord is throwing us both out. The police are here, and I'm in trouble."

After getting a load of the details, I assured Cathi that I would take Mom back immediately. Cathi packed up her stuff and moved in with my sister in North Charleston, and I took Mom home. But she was not the person I once knew. *I've got a crazy woman on my hands*, I thought. This was a week before Christmas.

Yes, my mom was "off her rocker," as they say, but she was actually happier than I had ever seen her.

She was like a child again. She was always smiling and had an easy charm about her. I hugged her and wept in her arms.

My mom developed her own unique dialog. She said stuff like, "Fred, the kitchen presser did the over, but I don't know if arms not can see the voter real estate." When friends visited, she approached them and said crazy things like that. We all couldn't help but laugh. But those few light moments belied a very grim existence for Mom. She constantly tormented herself, trying to perform tasks that didn't exist. I often watched her from the living room as she muttered to herself while repeatedly folding and unfolding clothes and bedspreads.

We had to put a child's gate in front of her bedroom door so she wouldn't wander outside or turn on the faucets and stove. Her memory lasted less than 10 seconds. She rarely had a lucid moment.

Connor, by now three years old and normally a very happy, fun-loving kid, felt very uneasy around my mom. He never wanted to enter her room. When he did, Mom would begin her strange talk, and Connor would become subdued and puzzled. I hated to have him exposed to this kind of thing on a daily basis.

But I felt so sorry for my mom. I couldn't even imagine what was running through her mind, such as it was. True, she was usually not aware of what was happening to her, but it was so hard to see this once very smart woman — who used to answer most of the questions on "Jeopardy," work at crossword puzzles daily, read novels regularly, and know the entire histories of baseball and football — reduced to this shell of a human being.

Still, I wouldn't have tried to put her in a nursing home — I felt I owed it to her not to let it come to that — except for the fact that she was incontinent with chronic diarrhea. This was truly horrible and gut wrenching. It was the worst thing with which I've ever dealt in my life. "Why, God, *why*?" I would scream as I cleaned the running feces from her legs and off the floor. Yes, at times like this even an agnostic starts to look for God.

One day I made the mistake of taking a nap and not checking on her for ninety minutes. I walked into her room, and shit was on the floor, the bed, the couch, the walls, the door, and the windows.

Of course, Mei, a former nurse who was not as quick at losing her marbles as I am, was perfectly calm during this storm. She just shrugged her shoulders and said, "Hey, we've got to take care of her until we can get help, so let's just do the best we can." I'll love Mei forever for her support during this most unpleasant time. She gave me strength.

But we did need a lot of help. I changed doctors because I didn't think the one we had been seeing cared enough about Mom. I asked him, point blank, "Can you please help us?" His reply was, "There's nothing I can do for you."

Fortunately, the new doctor I found was more sympathetic to our plight. He said he would fill out any papers needed to get her into a nursing home. But there's a lot of governmental red tape involved — obtaining Medicaid, getting Mom declared incompetent, and so forth — and moreover, most nursing homes in the area were always filled to capacity.

In the meantime, the doctor suggested Hospice, a group of dedicated caregivers, and I have to say they were like a band of descending angels. They supplied us with medicine, bed sheets, babysitting, advice, and hope.

But I knew it would take more than hope to get us out of this mess. It would take — dare I say it — prayer!

TWENTY FIVE
A TEMPLATE FOR LIVING

Mei believed in fate, God, and prayer. I believed in choice, taking action, and kissing on the first date. Mei would often say God helped us find each other. I would retort, "Or the Internet."

She was secure in her beliefs. I was not. For decades the big questions regarding the meaning of life and the very reasons for existence always bugged me. I wasn't so mind-boggled by an endless universe as I was the fact that there was even *one* proton. Why? Are we just a bunch of particles walking around? Does consciousness continue after the brain ceases to function? If there is a God, why all the suffering? And does Carmen Miranda's estate get royalties whenever people are read their Miranda rights?

Yep, I was full of questions. As I tried to cope with my mom's condition, I had sought answers in everything from the Bible to Isaac Asimov. Nothing made total sense until I studied near-death experiences (NDEs, for short).

Almost everybody has heard of NDEs. You know,

flatlining, "travel" through a tunnel toward a brilliant light, the feeling of being "home" again, meeting deceased relatives, feeling comfort, total peace and joy, told it's "not your time," etc.

Many scientists and doctors explain away NDEs by saying that the brain has a way of playing tricks on a person who endures severe trauma. We are being fooled by Mother Nature to make our "passing" as painless as possible.

But if NDEs are just hallucinations, the NDEers would return saying all kinds of random things like, "God told me to eat cheese" or "A giant turtle told me to kill nuns." But the majority of them come back preaching unconditional love and helping others.

I don't believe our minds at the time of death would trick us into "being nice."

Long story short, after reading hundreds of NDE stories and noting the many threads of truth they have in common, I, the ultimate skeptic who phoophooed everything metaphysical, had an *epiphany*. And I know an epiphany when I have one. The last time was in 1967 when Debbie Menard let me cop a feel.

The NDE phenomenon is real. *We live on after*

death, and what we do on Earth actually matters. I had found either "God" or an intelligent universe borne of love … whatever you choose to call it.

This was heavy stuff. I wasted no time expressing my newfound belief to Mei. Now it was I who was telling *her* about God.

She was highly receptive and wanted to learn more. I bought many books on spirituality and shared every bit of important information I could find with her. We were excited that we had this in common.

I also needed some help regarding Mei's relatives. If I couldn't change *them,* I would have to find a way to change *myself.* So I started reading a lot of self-help books and the philosophies of Deepak Chopra, Sakyong Mipham, Dr. Wayne Dyer, and even Dave Barry (well, you gotta laugh, too).

Quite to my own surprise, I began to study Buddhism, not as a way of life but just for inspiration. I reckoned the Buddha was the most enlightened man who ever lived. Fat but enlightened. Mei was so tickled that I was quoting Buddha to *her.*

The doctrines of Buddhism tell us to be of service

to others; to live in the moment; that life is a circle; there is no self; the only permanent thing is impermanence; don't think, *be*. That's why, after I began studying Buddhism, when Mei told me to take out the garbage, I always told her I couldn't — I was too busy *be*-ing.

My new awareness affected all aspects of my life. My approach to daily living was to lessen the negativity around me. If co-workers treated me like dirt, I didn't fire back, as I would have before. I would not only forgive them, I would try to find a way to make their day a little better.

I began to view others as divine creatures of God (yes, believe it or not, even Carrot Top is divine.) Much of the resentment I felt toward Mei's family melted away, replaced by patience and tolerance.

The change also brought me closer to my sister Cindy. She was already progressing in her spiritual — not religious — understanding. She even joined a Unitarian church, which dared to talk about reincarnation and karma. And I went to church with her! But I didn't stay because I was still uncomfortable with the hymns and hand holding. Plus there were NFL pre-games on. I said I became spiritual, not crazy. Regardless, my sister and I could now engage in long, inspiring conversations. It was quite a turnaround.

I now viewed my predicament with Mom as a life lesson, for me and for her. I no longer tried to run away from the problem — my new goal was to make her as comfortable and happy as possible, while still seeking the best possible care for her.

Mei and I began to pray, asking the universe to show us the path to help both Mom and us. To my surprise, the answers came very quickly. Doors opened that I thought were impossibly closed, people we didn't know reached out to help us, and within a few weeks Mom was placed in a very nice, well-run nursing facility close to our home. It didn't cost us a dime because she qualified for Medicaid.

We never felt we abandoned Mom, for we knew we couldn't have taken care of her by ourselves much longer. It was a question of our survival as a family. A tremendous burden was lifted from our hearts and minds, and I don't believe it would have happened so easily without spirituality.

Don't get me wrong. Life didn't suddenly turn into Mardi Gras. I would still have bad moments and bad days. But I now had a template for living.

TWENTY SIX
WE THAI ONE ON

I would never have imagined owning a restaurant. My father had owned several businesses, all of which failed. I saw how much of a hassle they were for him, and I believe his lack of business acumen ultimately contributed to his death — that, and a fast-moving bullet.

Besides, I always remembered that old saying: You don't own the business. *The business owns you.* Who needed such headaches?

But sometimes when a woman wants something badly enough, you just have to give in. Mei had been a waitress and cashier for several years. She certainly didn't see those things in her future. She wanted to have her own restaurant. I couldn't stand in her way. And, I must confess, despite my misgivings, the idea of being a restaurateur appealed to me.

We shopped around for a few months but couldn't find anything that we liked or could afford. There were opportunities to buy Chinese restaurants, but we both felt there were too many Chinese restaurants around town.

Then in May of '05, a friend of Mei's told her that she was in poor health and was planning to sell her business. This woman owned a Thai restaurant called Kanok's in North Charleston, where Mei had worked a couple of years previously. Once this woman sold her restaurant, she would then take the money back to her native Thailand to pay for much-needed surgery.

Mei and I had a long discussion about what it would take and what the risks would be if we tried to buy the restaurant. I basically told her this: "Mei, if the business fails, and we lose our home and wind up living in a camper, I still think we should go for it. You have to take chances in life to get anywhere. This is your dream, and I want to make it happen for you. Besides, it's not as big a risk as it seems because I still have a good job. We don't have to depend on the business to survive. Even if it takes months just to break even, it's okay. We can afford to be patient."

Mei couldn't argue with that. So, we secured a bank loan and bought ourselves a restaurant. Mei became the first Chinese person in Charleston to own a Thai restaurant. She couldn't believe she now owned a restaurant where she was a waitress only two years earlier.

And for me, it was doubly ironic. For more than twenty years I felt uncomfortable even entering a restaurant, as my first panic attack happened in a restaurant when I was nine years old. I did not eat in a restaurant from age nine to thirty-three. Now, at age fifty, I owned one.

All that sounds great, but really we were clueless about what we were getting ourselves into. Even though the chef, a world-class cooker of Thai cuisine, was staying on, and even though the previous owner promised she would help us out the first month during the transition, we were like babes in very big woods. We needed accountants, lawyers, and tax people. We had to get licenses, pay fee after fee, and jump through a dozen hoops. We even had to incorporate, forming an LLC (Limited Liability Company), to protect ourselves in case someone injured him/herself in our restaurant.

But before I realized all that, I thought, *How hard could this restaurant biz be?* One day I walked my blissfully ignorant self into an accountant's office and said, "I just bought a restaurant. What do I have to know?" Two and a half hours later, I emerged from the office a beaten man. I had no idea it took so much time, effort, and money just to own a small business.

I came home quite dejected and told Mei, "Honey, I can't handle this. I already have a full-time job, plus I have to watch Connor while you manage the restaurant. I don't have the time. You're going to have to handle the whole thing. I'll just be there for the heavy lifting."

Mei didn't mind that at all and threw herself into the operation 110 percent. I was really proud of the way she handled all the business affairs and also quickly learned the nuts and bolts of running a restaurant. She was Superwoman: at once manager, hostess, waitress, cashier, bartender, and cook.

But it was no longer Kanok's Resaurant, for we decided to change the name to Taste of Thailand. That didn't work out, however. We found out a new sign with a name as long as Taste of Thailand would cost us $5,000. Too many letters, you see. So we shortened it to Mei Thai, which only cost $1,800. Hey, as a businessman I've got to think about expenses.

We hired Mei's brother, Tom, to work in the kitchen. He had been a cook at several Chinese restaurants. His job initially was to help the chef, but he soon learned the art of Thai cooking and became an excellent chef himself.

But there was a catch. It is traditional for Asian

restaurants to provide housing for the staff (excluding the main chef, who was already being paid a fortune). Mei said we had to pay Tom an additional $700 for apartment rent. This sounded crazy to me, so I said, "Mei, I'd rather have your brother *live* with us than pay him an extra $700 a month."

Well, I guess that was exactly what Mei and Tom wanted to hear. So he moved in with us, permanently this time, and it was *my idea*!

It really wasn't a big deal, though. We had a spare room because Dan Dan was headed for Clemson University in upstate South Carolina. (I had *everything* to do with Dan Dan being accepted by Clemson. If not for my influence, she would certainly have made it to Harvard.)

The main drawback in owning a Thai restaurant, from my perspective, was the food. Remember, I'm a meat-and-potatoes guy. "Why didn't I buy a Ryan's?" I asked myself.

Just reading the menu items made me chuckle. Go ahead and read the following items out loud, and you'll see what I mean: *Poh Piah Sod*, *Khung Thod*, *Gai Pa Phrik*, *Larb*, *Moo Pad Phed*, *Ka-Nom Jean Nam Ya*, and *Mee Kok*.

At first they tried to give me curry, bean thread noodles, and some other thing that was so gross it didn't even *have* a name. Of course I would have none of that! But I managed to find at least five dishes on the menu that were not only tolerable, but also downright delicious. So I ate at the restaurant five nights week, rotating the same five dishes but saving tons on our grocery bill.

Suddenly, I had three jobs: designing pages at *The Post and Courier*, taking care of Connor (anyone who doesn't think that's a full-time job doesn't have kids), and helping out at the restaurant. While Mei and Tom did the bulk of the work, my job was simply to greet the patrons, make them feel at home, and handle any problems that might occur with the service.

They're right when they say you can't get good help nowadays. Often the waitresses we brought in were slow and/or dumb. We told one young gal, who had never worked as a waitress before, to make sure to wear comfortable shoes. So she returned the following morning in bedroom slippers. Also, we had to let one chef's helper go because he called in sick on a Monday. By itself, that's no biggie, but the reason he didn't make it to work was because he had sex with a hooker the entire weekend and was "too tired."

Every night after work at the newspaper I picked up Connor from day care, and we'd head for the restaurant. The regular customers looked forward to seeing him. They gave him hugs and bought him presents. But he often treaded the fine line between cute and annoying. For several weeks, Connor, by now totally corrupted by my geeky tastes in old monster movies, felt he needed to serenade customers with his version of "The Blob" (a cult '50s sci-fi film starring Steve McQueen). The lyrics, written by Burt Bacharach, no less, went something like this: "It creeps, it leaps, it slides and glides across the floor, right through the door and all around the wall; a splotch, a blotch, beware of The Blob." We lost several customers this way.

Our lives had gone from fairly simple to downright hectic. Mei stayed at the restaurant from 10:30 a.m. to 10 p.m. on weekdays, from 10:30 a.m. to 11 p.m. on Saturdays and from 4 p.m. to 9 p.m. on Sundays. Then, she would suddenly have to change those hours, as workers kept calling in sick and quitting on no notice. Sometimes she was able to go home on slow days and take a nap, or do a little shopping. But she was always exhausted by the time she came home, and she often went straight to bed. I guess this is the price you pay when you want to carve out a better future for yourself and your family. I knew that Mei was more than willing to pay that price.

Did we make any money those first few months? I'll put it this way: I quickly stopped looking at retirement villa brochures. Actually, we broke even, which is better than most neophyte business owners can say.

Yeah, we struggled. And all you have to do is clean gunk off tables at 11:00 p.m. to realize there is nothing glamorous about the restaurant biz.

But there was a bigger concern looming. We were growing apart again. Not only that, but people meet people in restaurants … people they perhaps should not meet.

TWENTY SEVEN
BY WHICH SIN, THE ANGELS FELL

Although the restaurant business can hurt any relationship, it hit ours hard. We had the cultural and language divides to start, multiplied by too much work and too little time for each other. Vacations were out of the question. Tensions rose.

Mei was also upset with me because, in her view, I wasn't pulling my weight. I argued that this was impossible since my weight was approaching the Chris Farley level, or at least half of it.

Even though I was working a full-time job and taking care of Connor, plus trying to develop a website called Neckbook, it wasn't enough. I guess I was too lazy and stubborn to put forth a greater effort. Whatever new enlightenment I experienced did not automatically make me want to vacuum and babysit every night.

One night I saw a laundry basket of washed but unfolded clothes in the living room. I didn't feel like folding them and putting them away, so I left them there. So did Mei. It became a test of wills. I don't perform very well on this kind of test. So the basket stayed there, untouched, for several days, until she couldn't stand it anymore and took care of it. (There's yet another ironic twist, involving laundry, that's coming up in just a few minutes of your reading time.)

The resentment I felt from Mei was palpable. She had no respect for me or my wishes. She asked if a Chinese friend of hers who was fired, and in a sense, homeless (though she could have gone back to China), could move into Dan Dan's room while she was away at college.

I gave a stern "*No!*"

We already had Tom there, as well as Mei's mom six months out of every year. I felt I had to draw the line. So what did I see when I came home from work the next day? The friend's stuff clogging up the garage. She had moved in. I didn't take it out on the friend, and I didn't have the heart to send her away. But Mei seemed to no longer care what I wanted.

And we weren't even sleeping in the same bed. I have always struggled with insomnia, which only got worse in those hectic times. I found I was getting only about four hours of sleep per night, but if I slept alone on the couch, I got at least six. Right or wrong,

I put a good night's sleep over Mei's loneliness in bed (though Connor slept with her).

I wasn't even there to hear the late-night calls she was getting from someone who was a stranger to me. Not that I would have understood the calls. He was Chinese, a truck driver who stopped by the restaurant often and listened to Mei's troubles. She was vulnerable. He was more than willing to make her happier.

I should have seen it coming. I knew Mei no longer loved me. So, I asked her directly: "Do you love me?" The best and most honest answer she could give me was, "I think so."

I kept thinking of leaving. I passed a residence hotel called InTown Suites on the way to work every day, and I imagined myself blissfully alone in a room without all the hassles of married life, family, and business. But I knew I couldn't break up the family. I would be devastated without Connor. Ironically, the InTown Suites would be the harbinger of our ending.

So as things got increasingly worse, Mei approached me in November 2006 about a separation. I wasn't surprised. But what did surprise me was that she said *she* wanted to move out. *She* wanted to be alone. Huh? That didn't sound right. Still, we hugged, and we both cried. She said she still loved me but not in a romantic way. She also said she would look for a place "of her own" soon.

Needless to say, I was pretty messed up at that point. I watched "Kramer Vs. Kramer," in which Meryl Streep leaves Dustin Hoffman alone to take care of their young son, and I cried like a baby.

But a part of me actually looked forward to being single again. Nobody wants to stay in a loveless marriage, even though I had not stopped loving her.

Still, the Greta Garbo "I want to be alone" bit made me wonder. Why would a woman want to leave her family? I'm sure she could live without me. But how could she live without Dan Dan and Connor?

My suspicions got more aroused when I noticed Mei would leave the house every Sunday around noon, her day off from the restaurant. I don't know where she went. I was too busy watching football to follow her.

Then, exactly at 3:00 p.m. on the first Sunday in December I received some life-altering information from a very close but unexpected source. Mei had been seen several Sundays at the InTown Suites with a man called Mr. A. Hole (not his real name).

That was all I needed to know. Fortunately, Mei didn't come back until 6:00 p.m., so I had three hours to calm down and think about things. This was difficult because it was during an "important" NFL game. In HD, no less. But I thought about what I wanted and how I could best achieve that. Those were the most important three hours of my life.

So this was why she wanted to "be alone." The sense of betrayal was like a dagger through my soul. A thousand more thoughts, a thousand more realizations, and finally I knew what to do.

When Mei walked in I confronted her immediately, but not with anger. "Tell me about Mr. A. Hole," I said. Then she confessed. I think she was relieved. She didn't have to hide and lie anymore. She simply asked, "What do you want?" It was the perfect question. I replied: "I want a divorce. You can have the house. You can have the restaurant. You can have the boyfriend. I just want Connor."

She answered: "Okay."

But don't judge Mei too harshly because she "gave up" her son. She didn't. She knew that Connor would never be happy away from me; she recognized the relationship we had as truly special. She even said, "I've

never seen a parent-child love as strong as yours."
She also knew the restaurant biz would not allow
her to take care of Connor day and night.

Actually, it was an almost noble sacrifice. She became the Streep character in the aforementioned
"Kramer vs. Kramer." In that film, Streep won custody. However, she knew it was best for the child to
remain with Hoffman.

In court in February of '07, the judge gave us joint
custody, though I was made the custodial parent.
I made sure Mei was aware she could see Connor
any time she wanted. I just wanted to make sure she
could never take him out of the state legally without
my permission.

So that was that. I lost my business, my home,
and my wife. Three weeks later my mom died. We
all have to deal with loss, but *c'mon*! How much can
one man take?

But let me say this period was hellish for the whole
family. I've never seen Dan Dan cry so much and so
hard. But you know what they say about silver lin-
ings? There was one. Dan Dan and I finally bonded.
When she came home from college for a month and
Mei had already moved out of the house and into an

apartment nearby, she asked if she could stay with me rather than with Mei and Mr. A. Hole. I agreed. I knew I hadn't been the best father to her, especially after Connor came along. I didn't treat her badly, but I didn't give our relationship the extra effort it needed. Thank God it wasn't too late to try to make up for that.

But Dan Dan and Connor weren't the only two people staying with me during this separation from Mei. Tom still lived in the house, and I swear this is true, *his ex-mother-in-law moved in*. They both stayed in Dan Dan's room while Dan Dan slept on the couch. This was totally awkward, so much so that the two of them just cowered in Dan Dan's room together for months (yes, *months*) and never came out! Or at least not when I was around.

I wanted to kick them to the curb and should have. But the "new me" prevented it.

Sometimes playing nice makes you a sucker. Like the time when, in the ironic twist I promised, I was doing Mei's laundry — yeah, that's right, I was doing the laundry of a woman who left me for another man because she didn't have a washing machine in her rented apartment — and I noticed I had just folded her lover's jockey underwear. Mei slipped them in! So I cut the crotch out and gave her the basket. An hour later she called me. She found the underwear and couldn't stop laughing.

But through all this foolishness I managed to keep my eye on the prize. Connor gave me the strength I needed to see this through. Having him at my side didn't make my life perfect. But it sure helped.

EPILOGUE

You can either let tragic losses destroy you, or you can move on and find something good in living, like cheese balls.

In the intervening years since the divorce, I bought a new home, which I share with my son. He spends the night with his mom at least once a week, and Mei and I have maintained a friendly relationship.

And, now it can be told: Mei is only part of her real name. She wanted my book to be published because she knew it was important to me. But she wanted to move on with her life, and she didn't want people coming up to her years later and asking her, "Are you the woman in this book?"

Eventually, she sold Mei Thai and opened a new restaurant in the West Ashley section of Charleston. She is no longer involved with Mr. A. Hole.

In no way do I think, as others have claimed, that Mei married me to attain the American dream and then left me in the dust once she got all she wanted from me. I know this woman. It's simply not in her character. The affair and divorce were not something she planned. She's a good person who made choices that had unfortunate consequences for the Smith family. But in retrospect, I made some bad choices myself. I can see how my behavior helped drive her away.

There are things about Mei and our marriage I'll always remember: Our first kiss. Teaching her to drive. Connor's birth. Her tremendous support during the most trying times of my mom's illness.

Her daughter Dan Dan graduated from Clemson University with high honors, and it's a privilege for me to still hear her call me "Dad."

From age six to age eleven, Connor was in a gifted class every year at Devon Forest Elementary in Goose Creek, and in 2011, he was named quarterback of his flag football team. He's huge. He weighed more at age eleven than I did when I was twenty. In 2012, he started at Westview Middle School.

I couldn't be more proud of him. He's even-tempered and compassionate. I hope to be just like him when I grow up. We watch NFL games together and listen to the Beatles. Of course, he had a hard time adjusting to the breakup, but now he seems healthy and happy.

As for me, I still have to keep my depression and

panic attacks under control. But they no longer define me. Being a single father does.

I haven't found that special someone (still looking for a sexpot who can stomach me), but I'll keep searching in between NFL seasons.

I've learned and un-learned a lot since I met Mei. I can only hope the overall experience has been enriching for her as well. I've seen some of the best and worst of China. The feeling I'm left with is this: There is no limit to what the people of that country can accomplish. Their worst enemy is themselves. But then that's true of all of us.

I'll close with a famous Beatles lyric from Abbey Road, the greatest album ever made: "And in the end, the love you take is equal to the love you make." I don't know exactly what it means, but it seems to fit.

ABOUT THE AUTHOR

Fred Lee Smith was born in Charleston, S.C., in 1954 and is not afraid to admit he has lived in the Lowcountry his entire life. He claims to have attended Charleston Southern University (then the Baptist College) long enough for there to be a record of some kind. You can check. Finding himself a dropout with nowhere to turn (except to his parents, with whom he lived and from whom he stole gas), Smith consulted a Quija board, which led him to *The News and Courier* newspaper in 1974. He intended to work there one month. Nearly forty years later, he's still there and somehow along the way, he managed to write more than 1,000 columns, reviews, and articles for the paper between 1978 and 1991. Shortly after *The News and Courier* and *The Charleston Evening Post* combined into *The Post and Courier* in the early 1990s, Smith dropped his writing pen — or rather, it was confiscated by editors who knew better — and began concentrating on page design. Fred is quoted as saying, "In that job, you don't have to take your work home with you, which was good for me because I had too much TV to watch."

He stumbled his way through several relationships ("at least one with an actual woman," he says) until he met Mei Li from China online in 1997. That experience, subsequent marriage, and numerous stupefying incidents comprise the subject of this merry memoir.